Hilma
from
Mother
Christmas 1934

THE CAMPFIRE GIRLS
ON THE PROGRAM

The
CAMPFIRE GIRLS
on the Program

OR

SINGING AND RECITING AT THE SENDING STATION

• •
•

By Margaret Penrose

Chicago
THE GOLDSMITH PUBLISHING CO.
PUBLISHERS

CONTENTS

CONTENTS

THE CAMPFIRE GIRLS
ON THE PROGRAM

Something Out of the Air
The Hurt Aviator
Not So Bad

THE CAMPFIRE GIRLS ON THE PROGRAM

CHAPTER I

SOMETHING OUT OF THE AIR

"OH, come on! We'll listen in on the radio concert, honey, and forget it," Amy Drew said soothingly.

"But she's so mean!" insisted Jessie Norwood. "So awfully mean!"

"Of course she is. Did you ever hear of anybody by the name of Ringold that wasn't mean? Not me!" And Amy tossed her head.

"But that does not do a bit of good," complained Jessie, her face still crimson and her eyes moist. "I cannot, Amy, overlook Belle's rudeness just because it runs in her family."

Amy giggled and sprang one of her jokes:

"Just because meanness runs in the Ringold family, like wooden legs," she said. "I know how you feel about that dress, Jess."

Jessie Norwood looked down at the frock she wore so daintily with eyes that were still clouded.

"If the Ringold's cook, as Belle says, has a

Sunday dress just like this I'll never want to wear it again. Not because her cook isn't just as good as I am," Jessie added quickly, as she chanced to see the expression on her chum's face, "but because Momsy bought the goods and had it made up by her own dressmaker, and it is supposed to be a little different from what you get in the ready-to-wear shops."

"Don't worry about it," Amy urged. "Belle's talk isn't as bad as the measles, or some other fell disease. Come on. If we catch the concert at four we'll hear Madame Elva; and you know she is the very best on the Stratford Electric Company's program."

The two Roselawn girls were walking up the boulevard from town on this July afternoon. The wide highway was speckled with broken bits of sunshine, patterned through the leaves of the tall elms. Now and then an automobile purred past the girls on one of the two oiled drives, or a horseman clattered by. Roselawn was distinctly the better suburban district of New Melford.

"We could have such nice times in our set," sighed Jessie, after a long minute, "if it wasn't for Belle Ringold and Sally Moon and their crowd. They are forever interfering."

"Static?" suggested Amy, grinning.

"No ether interference was ever as bad as Belle and Sally. See how they are annoying the boys about that moonlight box-party they have been trying to arrange for two weeks."

"The present moon will be quite worn out before they get around to the party," laughed Amy. "And, anyway, Darry and Burd have gone down to Barnegat to put the *Marigold* in commission again. If Belle holds off her moonlight party until they get back she'll wait till frost."

"Oh! You don't mean that the boys will stay away all summer, Amy?" cried her chum.

"No," rejoined Amy demurely. "I meant it will be a frost for Belle and Sally. Darry positively refuses to be roped in by Belle and her crowd."

"I never did feel like this about any other girl," Jessie Norwood confessed. "But I don't really believe there ever was such an unpleasant girl as Belle Ringold."

"Oh, yes, there must have been at least one," said Amy, the irrepressible, and giggling again. "Her mother, Mrs. Ringold, is beloved for the same virtues that endears Belle to us girls. Or, do I say 'we girls'?"

"You may say what you please—grammatically," replied Jessie, smiling again. "It is vacation, and even Miss Seymour has gone away. However, I suppose we should not criticise Belle's mother."

"Dear me, honey," groaned Amy. "You are so

good you make me ache. If Belle had spoken as nastily to me as she did to you, I would positively hate her and all her relatives."

"Look!" murmured Jessie Norwood suddenly. It was evident that she had not given much attention to her chum.

"Look! I thought from the way the radio sounded last evening that the aerial was twisted."

They were now in sight of the Norwood place, which was one of the show places of Roselawn. At one side an opening in the trees gave a view of Lake Monenset. Across the broad boulevard from the automobile entrance to the Norwood grounds, set upon another terraced lawn, was the Drew house, where Amy lived with her parents and her brother, Darrington Drew, when he was at home. The girls were high school pupils, but Darrington had just finished his first year at Yale.

Amy, staring in the direction her chum pointed, between the Norwood house and a tower at one side, shook her head with mock sadness.

"I really do believe, Jess," said she, "that there is something in the air besides static. There must be imps that twist those wires. You know it isn't a week since we lowered the whole thing and took the twists out."

"I don't suppose we really have more trouble with our radio than other amateurs. Come on,

Amy! Let's get into our working togs and do a good job while we are about it."

"All right," agreed Amy. "Lucky I left my radio suit over here."

"Your what?" asked her chum, laughing, as the two ran up the veranda steps.

"Radio suit," repeated Amy seriously. "Those overalls were once our farmerette costumes; but the war is over and the sword is beaten into a plowshare, and our farmerette overalls have become radio rigging suits. Whew! Don't go so fast, Jess. I can't climb stairs and talk at the same time."

In Jessie's bedroom the two girls changed to the overall suits Amy had mentioned. Young as Jessie Norwood was, she had a suite of rooms to herself. In the long sitting room was her radio cabinet, a much better set than the ordinary house instrument. It had a two-step amplifier and a horn, but there were the usual headphones as well.

"That concert is due right now," Jessie said, coming out into the big room. "Let us see how it sounds before we lower the aerial. It may have been partly static last night."

She opened the receiving switch and fastened on the head harness. Amy came over and sat down, likewise affixing one set of the phones. Jessie tuned the machine with practised hand. At first the chattering noises in the air meant nothing intelligible.

"But it's awfully loud," murmured the puzzled Amy. "Why, Jess! I never heard your set so loud."

"Goodness! That isn't radio," Jessie declared suddenly.

"Wha-a-at?" drawled the puzzled Amy.

"That's an airplane!" cried Jessie. "It must be coming right this way."

"Oh! Over the house!" gasped her chum. "It's zooming, Jess! Look!"

She tore the phone-tabs from her ears and darted to the window. Jessie could see out from where she sat. The noise of the aeroplane grew louder.

It was swooping so low that involuntarily the girls screamed.

"It—it will hit the house!" gasped Jessie.

"What can he be thinking of?" Amy demanded in equal amazement. "He is swooping so low——"

In seeming recklessness the aviator volplaned downward. Suddenly the roaring of the engine passed. If the pilot did not manage his controls within a dozen seconds in a way to shoot the plane upward again, there must surely be a catastrophe.

Jessie left her seat at the radio and thrust her head and shoulders out of the open window beside her chum. The nose of the plane continued to slant downward. The girls screamed again, for a wing of the plane struck the roof of the tower to which the farther end of the radio aerial was fastened.

"He'll be killed!" shrieked Jessie.

The plane seemed about to turn turtle. It crashed against the radio antenna and tore it from its fastenings. Then with a deafening crash the machine landed on the lawn, utterly wrecking one of the big rose gardens.

What had become of the reckless pilot the two girls at the window could not see.

CHAPTER II

THE HURT AVIATOR

THE two girls did not stand long at the open window of Jessie Norwood's sitting room. That crash of the airplane spurred them to excited activity.

Amy Drew led the way, and she led it shrieking. Mrs. Norwood appeared at the door of the library, demanding:

"What has happened, girls? Stop shouting, Amy, please! You will raise the neighborhood."

"That's what we want to do, Momsy!" Jessie cried. "Something dreadful has happened!"

"That radio set! I knew something would happen because of it," gasped the kindly but rather nervous woman.

In fact, when Jessie Norwood and her chum, Amy Drew, had first become interested in radio telephony Mrs. Norwood had been rather fearful of the new apparatus. Not that she would forbid her only child—nor would Mr. Norwood, who was a lawyer in New York—anything that might amuse her without doing others harm. But "Momsy," as Jessie always called her mother,

8

was very much afraid of lightning and she feared that the radio aerial would lead lightning, as well as radio broadcasting, into the house.

Jessie, however, although she had strung the aerial and set up the machine in her own room with very little help save what her chum gave her, had studied advisory radio books with care and had so placed and guarded the thing that there was positively no danger from lightning.

Indeed, so careful was she, and quite by instinct now, that before she had left the room to run down to see what had happened to the fallen airplane pilot, she had closed the receiving switch. And there was not a cloud in the sky!

Roselawn people had become vastly interested in radio telephony since Jessie Norwood had got her outfit. The Norwoods were popular anyway, but since the church bazaar, which had been held on the Norwood lawn on the recent Fourth of July, Jessie found herself more than usually sought after.

At that time, and by her suggestion, a tent had been raised upon the lawn and her radio set disconnected, brought down into the tent, and linked up again with the aerial. The tent seated a hundred people, and it was filled to capacity at each show. Immediately radio telephony became "all the rage," Amy said, "all over Roselawn."

The practical uses of the new interest were not alone discovered in the first volume of this series, called "The Radio Girls of Roselawn"; but through radio, or because of it, the two chums and their friends fell in with a wealth of adventure.

Associated with Jessie and Amy in the incidents of the former book were Amy's older brother, Darrington, and his college friend, Burd Alling. And for the very reason that these young men were older than the high school girls, some of the classmates of the latter were convinced that they should likewise have the privilege of chumming with the two collegians.

Belle Ringold, a girl not far from the age of the radio girls of Roselawn, but who dressed in a fashion much older than her years, had shown her spleen on this very day by saying something very unpleasant regarding Jessie's dress.

Jessie had quite forgotten this, however, as she plunged down the stairway and out of the door after Amy.

The wrecked plane looked a ruin. Every part of it seemed to have been torn to bits. Both wings were twisted into scraps and the woodwork was splintered into matchwood. It did not seem, to the horrified eyes of the two girls, that any human being could have come down in that plane and lived.

Amy halted on the top step of the wide porch, clasping her hands.

"Oh, Jess!" she groaned. "That bed of beautiful Marshal Niel roses your mother thought so much of!"

Jessie knew that her chum was too excited to realize just how this sounded. The roses—the whole great bed of them—were uprooted and crushed. But there was greater disaster than that.

"The pilot! The pilot, Amy!" Jessie gasped. "He must be killed."

"If he didn't get out before the crash, he must be," rejoined Amy.

"Goodness! How could he get out?"

Jessie was ahead. She ran to the far side of the heap of rubbish that was the collapsed aeroplane. There seemed no part of the machine left intact. And just as the girls reached the spot a curl of smoke ascended from the midst of the wreck.

"It's on fire! Oh, Amy, the thing will be burned up! And the poor man!"

"Oh, he mustn't!" groaned Amy.

Jessie suddenly saw an arm sticking out from under some of the lighter wreckage. It was clothed in the olive-drab uniform coat of an aviator. She seized the gauntleted hand and began to tug with all her strength.

"Where are you going, Amy?" she cried. "Come and help me."

"Going to get the lawn hose. We'll put out the fire, Jess."

"But let's get this man out first. He may roast while you are wetting down the plane with the hose."

This seemed practical even to Amy. She lent her strength to Jessie's and fortunately they were able to drag the unconscious pilot forth. He wore the usual helmet, the tabs of which were fastened over his ears. It was plain that he had been up to a high altitude before making this unfortunate swoop that had ended so disastrously.

"Is he dead? Oh! is he dead?" murmured Jessie Norwood.

"Oh, I hope not," gasped her chum. "Who is he? Anybody we know, Jess?"

Jessie waved her away. "Run for Chapman or the gardener. Where can they be? Let them get out the hose and put out this fire. Do, Amy!"

"I'll do that myself," declared the other girl. "I thought of it first," and away she went to where the hose was reeled beside the house-plug.

Mrs. Norwood had come out on the veranda, and, seeing that the girls were doing all they could, had herself gone in search of Chapman or the gardener. Jessie unfastened the aviator's helmet and carefully removed it.

One look at the face of the victim of the accident, and the girl emitted a scream that startled her mother, just then coming around the corner of the house.

"For pity's sake, child!" she cried. "Is it as bad as that? Come away, Jessie. Here comes Chapman. Let him attend to it!"

Chapman ran hastily to the spot—just in time, in fact, to get the stream of water from the hose right between the shoulders. Amy was rather reckless with the hose. But she soon got it trained upon the burning petrol tank. That scattered the flames at first, but in the end it extinguished the fire.

Chapman, meanwhile, leaned above the injured pilot and began an examination of his body. The victim remained unconscious, and Jessie continued to stare at his pale countenance, not offering to help the chauffeur in his examination. She had recognized the young man lying there on the ground.

"Oh, Momsy! it's Mark Stratford," the girl murmured. "Poor Mark! What will his father do if he's killed?"

" 'The millionaire kid'," the chauffeur said, kneeling beside the injured pilot. Nor did he use the nickname given to Mark Stratford by his college chums in any tone of scorn. The heir to the great Stratford estate, as well as to the controlling interest in the Stratford Electric Company at Stratfordtown, was well liked by everybody who knew him. Then Chapman added: "It's a bad tumble he took, Miss Jessie; but he ain't dead."

"Chapmain," said Mrs. Norwood, "you and Bill bring him in. We will take him up to bed." She started the women servants to making indoor preparations. She, too, knew the millionaire's son and liked him.

"Jessie," Mrs. Norwood commanded her daughter, "go to the 'phone and telephone to Doctor Ankers. Perhaps you had better call Doctor Sefert, too."

"Yes, Momsy. And I'll get Stratfordtown on the line and tell somebody there—somebody of the family, I mean."

Jessie and her mother hurried in ahead of the men bearing Mark Stratford. Amy, having extinguished the fire and now having nothing better to do, followed after, carrying the discarded flying helmet.

Jessie ran at once to the telephone. "It would be great," she thought, "if we had a sending instrument as well as a receiving radio set. We could broadcast the news of Mark's accident and his family would get it promptly."

However, she had enough to do during the next few minutes calling the two doctors and telling them what was wanted of them and urging the necessity for haste. It took longer to reach the Stratford home beyond Stratfordtown. And there Jessie could talk only with a servant whose sympathy, if he felt any, for his young master's case was hidden behind the unemotional exterior of the well-trained English servant.

She knew that Mark Stratford had no mother, and although his father and his other relatives might consider him the apple of their eyes, they were not likely to influence him against taking risks. Mark, had he had a mother, would possibly, for her sake, have been a little less reckless in his activities as an aviator after the war was ended.

"And just see what has come of it, poor fellow," murmured the Roselawn girl, as she hung up the receiver and enclosed the telephone instrument again in the bisque doll which housed it on the hall table. "Suppose he is killed or seriously hurt? Dear, dear! What a frightful tragedy!"

"It's all of that," half sobbed Amy, who was standing behind her chum. She dabbed her eyes with her handkerchief. "And your radio antenna, Jess, is completley wrecked."

"I have always been afraid that that racer would bring him to grief."

"Look! Look!" gasped Amy hysterically. She pointed to the wreck of the aeroplane. "He—he was driving that."

"What under the sun was it?" murmured Mr. Stratford. Then, suddenly, he realized the nature of the wreck. "Not the plane?"

"Yes, Mr. Stratford," Jessie interposed. "He fell with that thing. But, as I tell you, Doctor Ankers and Doctor Leffert say they can find nothing very serious the matter with him."

There was a quizzical twist to the corners of Mr. Stratford's lips as there was to Mark's. Jessie thought that he must be just as likable as his son was. And now that he was reassured about Mark's accident and his condition, he gave more attention to the two girls.

"You are Robert Norwood's girl, I have no doubt?" he said to Jessie. "You have some look of your father. I have met him on the Country Club links."

"Yes, sir, I am Jessie Norwood," Jessie said, flushing a little. As she expressed it to Momsy, she just *would* blush, no matter who spoke to her! "And this," Jessie added, turning to her chum, "is Amy Drew, who lives across the street."

"And belongs to Wilbur Drew, I have no doubt?"

"Only half, if you please," Amy said demurely. "Mrs. Sarah Drew likewise claims a share in me."

Mr. Stratford seemed much amused by this statement. But he turned with some impatience toward the house door. Mr. Norwood was just coming out.

"Glad you are here, Mr. Stratford," said the lawyer. "They tell me the boy has been asking for you. The consensus of opinion is that shock and a general shaking up is about the worst that has happened to him."

"He always was a lucky young scamp," replied Mr. Stratford. "And if there is a reckless thing to do, he'll find it. Yet I'm sort of proud of him, Norwood. There aren't many boys of his age that have done the things he has."

"I grant you that," said Mr. Norwood, yet doubtfully. "Just the same," and he pinched Jessie's ear, who stood beside him, "I am glad my son is a girl."

"Ha, ha!" laughed Mr. Stratford. "I have been noticing that both these girls seem to be aping the boys pretty closely as to dress. And very fetching costumes they are."

"Oh!" exclaimed Amy, with vast coolness (Jessie was for the moment confused), "we have to clear up Jessie's radio aerial and hang it up again. That old aeroplane smashed right through it when it fell. That is how we come to be wearing our radio suits, Mr. Stratford."

She tucked her hand in the crook of her chum's elbow and led her away. They heard the gentlemen laughing as they went indoors. Jessie was secretly very glad that her father and Mr. Stratford *could* laugh. Suppose Mark had been killed!

"Mrs. Norwood says that you and Mark are perfectly welcome here," Mr. Norwood said to the senator. "If the doctors think he should remain, I think you had better leave him."

Both Dr. Ankers and Dr. Leffert had stayed to confer with the father of the injured young man. After this conference it was decided that an ambulance should be sent for and Mark removed to his own home. He asked for the girls and seemed to feel that somehow he owed them something for smashing the radio antenna.

"I'll make it up to you, Miss Jessie," was one of the last remarks he made as they carried him out of the house that evening. "It's a shame you should have all that trouble because of me."

Jessie stood on the veranda as the ambulance rolled away and gravely announced:

"Do you know what I just wish, Amy Drew?"

"I haven't the first idea. Wish for a million; then if you get it, we'll go fifty-fifty."

"Nothing so common as that," pursued Jessie, with continued gravity. "Money isn't everything in this world. No," she went on. "My thought is of something entirely different. I just wish——"

"So you do. What is your wish, honey?"

"If Mark Stratford thinks he owes us something for tumbling down here and smashing our aerial, I wish he would make it up to us in just one way."

Amy arched her brows and looked curiously at her friend. "I don't get your meaning at all, Jess," she said.

"Why, we've talked enough about it, Amy. It is in his power—and in his father's power—to do us the greatest favor."

"Goodness me, Jess! It *must* be a million dollars you are talking about."

"Nothing of the kind," returned Jessie. "I should think you would see what I mean. We have talked enough about it. Think! If they would only ask Mr. Blair, their radio superintendent, to let us sing and recite on the Stratford program. Wouldn't that be fine?"

"It certainly would be scrumptious," Amy agreed. "I never! Why can't we ask him the very next time we see Mark? Mr. Stratford, I mean."

"Oh, I shouldn't like to do that. We don't know Mark's father well enough."

"How well have we got to know him to ask?" demanded Amy.

"We-ell, he might not like it. But if Mark says anything again about feeling that he has put us to trouble about the wires, I shall feel just like asking *him*."

"Pooh!" exclaimed Amy. "I'll not only feel like asking him, but I will do so. Why not? He's only a boy like Darry. I'm not afraid of any boy."

The Lost Watch
The Hospital Drive,
Belle Sniffs at It

CHAPTER IV

THE LOST WATCH

I T was, after all, too late that evening to do any repairing of Jessie's radio antenna. The girls had changed back into their ordinary wear for dinner. That meal at the Norwood house was set back an hour or more because of the confusion attending the wreck of the airplane and the departure of the Stratfords in the private ambulance.

The exciting incidents of the evening were not concluded by the departure of the injured Mark and the despatch of dinner. As the Norwoods came out upon the lighted porch they heard voices on the lawn near the wrecked aeroplane.

"Who is Chapman shooing off the place?" asked Mrs. Norwood of her husband.

"Neighborhood children, I suppose," said Jessie's father carelessly. "Come to see the wreck. Better not let them stay to-night—Mr. Stratford said he would send a truck and men to pick up the pieces in the morning—for there are small parts of the plane that might be carried away by inquisitive boys."

"Oh, Daddy, that isn't a boy!" Jessie suddenly declared, and darted down the steps.

The chauffeur had evidently been peremptory in his remarks to the uninvited callers. A shrill voice replied to Chapman's warning:

"You needn't be so grouchy about it. We wouldn't carry off anything. It ain't no good, anyway—not even for kindling. We just wanted to look at it."

"Well, now you've seen it, beat it," growled out Chapman.

"Ain't we going?" demanded the same sharp voice. "We seen the old thing fall from clear over to Dogtown, and we jest wanted to see if it did any damage to Miss Jessie's wires and things. And it did."

"Oh, Henrietta!" cried Jessie, running across the lawn. "Don't go. We haven't seen you for a week."

"And you ain't going to see me for another, if that man is going to chase us off your place, Miss Jessie," said the sharp little voice. "We wasn't doing anything."

"Of course you weren't, Henrietta," agreed Jessie. "And Chapman did not understand."

"Oh, I understand all right, Miss Jessie," the chauffeur said. "I know those Dogtown kids."

"Be careful!" commanded Jessie, warmly. "You know I am fond of Henrietta, Chapman."

"Well, maybe she is all right," said the man grudgingly. "But those others——"

"Ain't nobody here but Charlie Foley and the Costello twins and Montmorency Shannon, and me," declared Henrietta promptly. "Who does he think is a thief, I'd like to know?"

"Now, Henrietta!" admonished Jessie. "That isn't nice, and you know it. You mustn't meddle with any part of the broken aeroplane, for the man who owns it is going to come for it to-morrow and will want all the parts."

"They were poking around in the ruins all right," grumbled Chapman, moving away.

"If he thinks I took anything, he can search me," said one of the Dogtown boys.

Jessie did not know which one spoke. She never had been able to distinguish between them. But by this time she should have been pretty well acquainted with Henrietta Haney and her friends.

The Roselawn radio girls had become acquainted with this queer, little, half wild and wholly untaught child through certain odd circumstances related in detail in "The Radio Girls of Roselawn"; and Henrietta had proved to be both an amusing and a helpful child. She was particularly enamored of Jessie Norwood because of the latter's kindness to her, and because Jessie had aided in recovering the freedom of Henrietta's cousin, Bertha Blair, who had been restrained illegally so that she might not testify in an important court case in which Jessie's father was interested.

It was of Bertha Blair that the Roselawn girl now questioned little Henrietta.

"Did Bertha go to see that lady about a place, where she could have you with her, Henrietta?"

"She went once, but the woman was out. And when we went the second time, Billy Foley had burned a hole in my nice silk dress and my stockings got tored, and I looked a sight. So the lady says: 'Who's that awful little thing you've got with you, girl?' So we didn't get that job."

"Oh, dear, me! How unfortunate," sighed Jessie. "And Mrs. Curtis really wanted young people about her. The doctor said it would be the best thing in the world for her."

"Huh!" said the abrupt Henrietta. "She didn't want any raggety kid like me. I was sorry about the taffeta silk, Miss Jessie."

"I am sorry, too, that you were not more careful," Jessie told her. "How did Billy come to burn the dress?"

"With a hot poker. I was back to him. And he burned a patch of *me,* too!"

Had Amy Drew heard that she would have screamed. But Jessie knew that the odd little Henrietta had no intention of being comical. The hole burned in the only silk dress she had ever owned was a tragedy to Henrietta's mind.

"Can't it be mended?" Jessie asked.

"I tried to. But I've only a piece of yellow silk and that don't match very well," sighed the child.

"I should say not!" gasped Jessie. "The taffeta is blue."

"And I can't sew small stitches," confessed Henrietta. "I try, but I bungle, Mrs. Foley says."

"Wouldn't Mrs. Foley mend the dress for you?"

"She would if she could find the time. But you know how it is yourself—with six kids, and all of 'em boys, and a man that drinks."

Jessie remembered to tell that to Amy the next morning when she ran over early to begin the radio repairs. Again the chums were in the overall suits that Mr. Stratford had joked about.

Men from Stratfordtown, with a big autotruck, had already arrived to remove the débris of the smashed plane. From under the débris Chapman and the gardener had rescued most of the radio antenna. But Jessie saw at once that the aerial would have to be entirely rearranged, and some new wire added.

"We will put it up differently this time, anyway," she said to Amy, but the latter asked, complainingly:

"Wasn't the other way good enough? I am sure we heard the concerts and other things from the broadcasting stations all right. Think how nicely it worked when the ladies of our church gave the bazaar here and you rigged the receiving set in the tent."

"I don't mean to change the rigging to aid in the distinctness of our receiving," said her more enthusiastic friend. "But you know Momsy has always been a little afraid of lightning striking the house because of the tangle of wires outside."

"He, he!" chuckled Amy. "Remember how the Stanley boys got into trouble rigging their set in that thunderstorm and we thought the minister's house was on fire?"

"I do. And wasn't it ridiculous?" Jessie observed. "But I read of a way to rig the antenna which will make a positive 'lightning break,' and I want to look it up in the magazine and see if I can use the idea."

"But," proclaimed Amy, who objected to any additional work, "if you are always careful to close the switch at the set there is never any danger from lightning."

"But Momsy will feel happier if I do this. She said so last night," and Jessie nodded a determined head. "There!" She heard her mother calling. "I wonder what she wants?"

"I hope she wants two George Washington

sundaes brought from the Dainties Shop," declared Amy, eagerly, following her friend toward
the house.

"And would you go for them in this costume?"
laughed Jessie.

"We-ell, I'm fond of sundaes," confessed the
impish Amy.

"Oh, girls," Mrs. Norwood greeted them.
"Think how unfortunate! Mr. Stratford's sec-
retary has just telephoned me, and——"

"You don't mean, Momsy, that Mark is not
so well?" Jessie interrupted.

"No. It is not that. Mark is hard to keep
in bed this morning, Mr. Theron says. But he
misses his watch—that beautiful diamond-set
hunting-case watch that you have seen him wear."

"Momsy!" cried Jessie. "That handsome
watch that his grandmother gave Mark when he
returned from France?"

"Yes. It really is a misfortune. But I wonder that his clothes were left on him when he
came down with such a crash, let alone his watch,"
said Mrs. Norwood. "Now we shall have to
search all around here——"

"But surely, Mrs. Norwood, it was not lost
inside the house—when they took off his clothes to
put him to bed, for instance?" Amy said wonderingly.

"Quite true. We know he must have dropped

it when the plane landed. But it might have been flung fifty feet away when the machine came down with such a crash."

"Oh, Momsy!" exclaimed Jessie. "Or it might be buried in the dirt of the rose garden where the plane landed. I'm going to look. Come on, Amy!" and Jessie ran down the veranda steps again.

Amy was right at her shoulder when her friend reached the place between the house and the tower where the aeroplane had fallen. The men had now removed everything but some worthless bits of the machine. The rose bushes were flattened, and the sod was torn up for some yards around. That part of the Norwood place would not look as it had before until the next season.

"Now, let's look carefully, everywhere," Jessie said. "Those workmen, of course, would not find the watch and say nothing about it?"

"They came from Stratfordtown, and I'm sure they are fond of Mark," said Amy reflectively. "They say everybody is fond of Mark over there, and proud of him, too."

"Then the watch must be here," Jessie declared.

"Perhaps," her chum said, with continued gravity. "But what you just told me about little Hen and those Dogtown kids being up here last evening and poking around, gives me a worried thought, honey."

"Oh, Amy! Little Henrietta? Never!"

"Perhaps not," said her friend. "And we haven't begun to look for Mark's watch yet. But just the same, I believe Chapman was quite right in chasing them away from the plane, as you say he did."

"Oh, but I would never believe such a thing of Henrietta," declared Jessie Norwood. "Never in this world."

CHAPTER V

THE HOSPITAL DRIVE

"REALLY, girls, unless you were moles, you could scarcely have searched more faithfully for Mark's watch," Mrs. Norwood said, coming out to preside over the activities of Jessie and Amy.

"What *do* you suppose has become of the thing?" sighed her daughter.

"I've dug my fingernails full of dirt. Manicuring will never repair the ravages of it," Amy said ruefully, looking at her hands.

The rubbish left from the wrecked plane had all been removed. The workmen from Stratfordtown had seen nothing of Mark's lovely watch. Although it was rather an old-fashioned piece of jewelry for a young man to wear, the girls knew that it was very valuable. But it was the associations connected with the gift that made it particularly valuable in the consideration of the senator's injured son.

"It is too bad," sighed Jessie again. "Mark was almost killed by his tumble, and now he must give up his watch."

"Say!" drawled Amy. "Did you ever think that he has lost his nice shiny aeroplane, too? That is scarcely worth carting back to Stratfordtown. I heard one of the men say so."

"Have you looked everywhere for the watch, girls?" Mrs. Norwood asked. "I dread telephoning over to tell him that we cannot find it."

"Maybe we would better look again," Jessie observed doubtfully.

"But you have already dug over the whole garden. My poor Marshal Niels!" murmured her mother.

"It is no use," declared Amy, with briskness. "Somebody came along and picked it up."

"Oh! Don't say that!" cried Jessie.

"It might be so," her mother observed. "There have been people around to view the wreck. Those children, for instance, last evening."

"That's just what I said; but Jess won't hear to it," Amy cried. "We don't know how honest those Dogtown kids are."

"Little Henrietta is no thief," Jessie declared earnestly.

"I don't believe she is, either," her mother said, smiling. "That funny little thing could not possibly be mean, if she is untamed. But those children with her—especially those boys. A watch such as this that has been lost would be a great temptation."

"But, Momsy! They would not even know the value of it."

"Leave it to Henrietta, or to Montmorency Shannon," said Amy quickly. "That Shannon boy doesn't have to be led about by a little dog," and Amy laughed again.

"Of course he is smart enough," agreed Jessie. "But being smart and poor does not prove his dishonesty," she added severely.

"That is true, Jessie," her mother said approvingly. "Poverty does not walk hand-in-hand with dishonesty by any manner of means. And the poor need our help in any event. That is what we are trying to establish the new hospital for. That fund is worrying me," and the good woman sighed.

"It's a far cry from Mark's watch and Montmorency Shannon to the New Melford's Women's and Children's Hospital," laughed Amy, immediately recovering her spirits.

"And a still farther cry to our new aerial," Jessie said. "Come, Amy, there is no use grubbing here any more. We might as well get to work erecting the wires again. I know where there is part of a roll of number fourteen wire in the garage. We'll need some of that."

"Radio?" said Mrs. Norwood, hesitatingly. "I wonder, Jessie, if that isn't the way to help us out?"

"What do you mean, Momsy?" her daughter asked.

"The hospital fund need is on my mind. If we could give some new entertainment by which to raise money—and what is newer than radio?"

"Radio telephony is not exactly new," Jessie said reflectively. "You know that, Momsy. But I suppose we could give a radio entertainment again. It would not be exactly new——"

"Oh! Oh!" cried Amy Drew suddenly, and she pirouetted about on the torn sward and clapped her hands.

"My dear Amy," laughed Jessie, "has something bitten you?"

"Exactly," agreed the excited Amy. "And it is an awful bite—believe me!"

"That sounds very much like slang to me, Amy," laughed Jessie's mother. "What do you mean? What is it that has bitten you?"

"An idea," replied Amy energetically. "And the finest ever! Listen, folkses!"

"Do tell us, dear," said her chum warmly.

"At the bazaar, you know," Amy said earnestly, "Jess just connected up with whatever chanced to be coming through the ether. It was bits of program from all over. But why not have a regular program—a big one—broadcasted from one station for the special purpose of attracting attention to your drive for the hospital fund, Mrs. Norwood?"

"I don't just see, Amy——"

"I do! I do!" cried Jessie delightedly. "Oh, Momsy, don't you see? Get big singers like Madame Elva, and other musicians, and all those interested in your hospital. Then find some sending station where they will let you give the concert——"

"The Stratford Electric Company," interrupted Amy.

"Good! Fine!" crowed Jessie.

"Can such a thing be done?" asked the wondering Mrs. Norwood, who had a rather confused idea of the uses of radio telephony.

"Of course it can be done, Momsy. It is a wonderful idea. Think! Thousands and thousands of people will be listening in."

"But won't the concert have to be given in a hall—like your entertainment in the tent?"

"Nothing like that, Momsy," declared her energetic daughter. "Understand that if you get your entertainers together at a certain hour at the sending station—say eight o'clock in the evening—and arrange to have them sing and play and recite just as though the audience were before them, you will be able to get many, many people to listen in who understand that, although they are getting a free concert, it is one to advertise the need of the New Melford Women's and Children's Hospital."

"Oh! How ingenious you two girls are," said Mrs. Norwood with more than slight approval. "But do you suppose the people who have radio sets will understand?"

"They will if there is not too much atmospherics," Amy said, grinning.

"Stop joking, Amy. Don't spoil it all," cried Jessie. "You have started a perfectly fine idea. And we must help Momsy carry it out."

"Oh, my dears," Mrs. Norwood hastened to say, "you must understand that I cannot decide this thing myself. I am only one of the committee. But it does seem as though Amy's thought were really inspired."

"That's all the thoughts I have—the inspired kind," declared Amy gravely. "And they are at your service, Mrs. Norwood."

That was the start of it. Mrs. Norwood began calling up the other ladies of the hospital fund committee and explaining Amy's idea to them. She really forgot, for the time, that she was supposed to report to Stratfordtown that Mark's beautiful watch was not to be found anywhere about the Norwood premises.

"And do you suppose," said Jessie to her chum, in a worried tone, as they set to work to string again the radio antenna, "that somebody picked up that watch Mark lost? I hate to think any one about here would steal it."

"What do you mean—steal it?" asked Amy briskly. "If it was merely picked up—why, I would do that myself. I certainly would not leave a diamond-studded watch lying on the ground. Not much!"

"But you would not pick it up and walk off without saying anything about it," objected Jessie. "No, you wouldn't. And nobody else who really was honest."

"Well, those kids from Dogtown don't know as much about honesty as we do, I suppose."

"I don't want to believe such a thing about them, especially about little Henrietta."

"She's awfully cute, I admit," said Amy. "But after all, we do not know just how good she is."

Jessie sighed. The very reason why she would not admit the possibility of Henrietta's knowing anything about the lost watch was based on this point that Amy had brought up. They did not know much about Henrietta Haney's moral character, and nothing at all of the characters of the children she associated with at Dogtown.

"It seems reasonable that the lost watch would be a great temptation to any of those kids who were poking about the wrecked aeroplane last night," said Amy, after a pause in the conversation, during which the girls were busy with the antenna.

"A whole lot of things that are reasonable aren't true," responded Jessie, a little sharply for her.

"Yes, and a whole lot that are unreasonable are true, I suppose," agreed her chum.

"Anyway, I don't believe, and I don't intend to believe unless I have to, that little Henrietta or any of her friends had anything to do with the disappearance of that watch. So there!" And Jessie went on with her work rather grimly.

CHAPTER VI

BELLE SNIFFS AT IT

THE Junior League of the Church held a business meeting that afternoon, and Jessie and Amy, having completed the restringing of the aerial and, as Amy said, opened communication again with the ether, the two chums walked downtown to the parish house. Dr. Stanley's church with the parsonage on one side and the parish house on the other, faced Bonwit Boulevard, but it was only on the edge of Roselawn. His was a large parish.

This latter fact was the reason why Belle Ringold and most of her friends attended the same church, as well as the same day school, as Jessie and Amy. The former girls lived nearer to New Melford proper. Naturally, among the young people, there was some little rivalry between the Roselawn circle and these others.

On this afternoon the main topic of discussion was of the interest the church societies were bound to take in the new hospital. All clubs and institutional societies were bound to lend a hand in so noble a work as this proposed. Dr. Stanley had spoken more than once from the pulpit of the proposed raising of a foundation fund for the hospital.

"Oh, we've got to do something, of course," Belle Ringold said rather crossly. "It's expected. But I do think that we girls ought to have our time to ourselves between school terms."

"Why, it will be fun," said Amy, overhearing this complaint. "How do you want to spend your time this summer, anyway, Belle?"

"Not working like a regular slave in some show or bazaar, or some other money-making scheme. Of course, you younger girls don't mind. You have few social duties——"

"My! My! Hear ye!" chuckled Amy, who seldom got offended by them but always made fun of Belle's airs. "Whom are you entertaining, Miss Ringold? The Prince De Kakyak? Your time is so fully occupied, I know. Oh, de-ah, yes!"

Jessie pulled her chum's sleeve in warning while Belle's eyes flashed.

"Miss Impudence!" she said. "You ought to be in the nursery still."

"Believe me," said the incorrigible girl, grinning, "I never was very still in the nursery, or anywhere else. However, fearing that if I kept still now you would have a misapprehension concerning what the hospital committee means to do about raising the fund and the proposed entertainment, I will a tale unfold——"

"Pooh! What do you know about it?" scoffed Belle.

"Well, I ought to know a good deal. It was my idea," Amy said proudly. "Wasn't it, Jess?"

"I'd like to know what you mean?" exclaimed Belle, heatedly. "You can't fool me."

Jessie felt called upon to support her chum. Besides, it was true. Amy had really suggested the radio concert idea. She said so.

"Well!" ejaculated Belle Ringold, "if they think that I am going to be at the beck and call of you girls of Roselawn and help boost one of your schemes, I guess not!" and she sniffed audibly.

"Don't be so sour, Belle," laughed Amy. "Did anybody ask you to do anything about it?"

"I guess you don't know everything," Sally Moon said quickly, catching at a chance to make her friend feel a little better. "You may have started this radio concert idea, but it isn't finished yet. Do you know what Miss Allister wants?"

"Something pretty good, I expect," said Amy easily. "Miss Allister is awfully nice, if anybody should ask you."

"Well," said Sally, eagerly, delighted to be able to tell news in order to counteract the effect of the Roselawn girls' statements, "Miss Allister has asked the chorus that sang at graduation and made such a hit, to repeat the numbers at this radio concert you seem to know so much about."

"Well, I never! Is it going to be an amateur affair?" exclaimed Amy, with some scorn, and with more than a little disappointment, too.

"I think that is splendid," declared Jessie. "You girls that were in that chorus will have an interesting time. I wonder what sending station will arrange for giving the concert?"

"I never!" repeated Amy, still pouting a little. Then she laughed shortly and the usual sunny look came into her pretty face. "Well," she confessed, "I guess our idea has got clear away from us. We're not in it, Jess. We neither of us sang in Miss Allister's chorus."

"But where will the concert be given?" her chum repeated, looking for an answer to Sally Moon.

"At Stratfordtown. So we just heard. The committee has arranged to send the stuff from there. And say, Jess! Was it really Mark Stratford who fell in his plane over at your place yesterday?"

Amy groaned heartily while her friend replied affirmatively to the question of Sally Moon.

"And I'll say he fell into luck," said Amy. "He lost a million dollar airplane, more or less, and a diamond-set watch that he thinks the world of, and didn't even break a finger. But here am I, wasting gray matter on thinking up schemes for the hospital committee to use in raising money, and then cheated out of having any share in the radio concert. Jess! do you hear what these girls that belong to Miss Allister's chorus are going to do?"

"I am glad for their sakes," said Jessie composedly. "Perhaps we can get into it, too, Amy."

"Not with us!" snapped Belle Ringold, who had by no means got over her grouch. "If you two try to get into that chorus, I won't sing at all. And I know others that feel the same."

"You all—you and your friends—must feel awfully uncomfortable," laughed Amy. "I would not have those feelings for worlds, Belle."

"Never mind," whispered Jessie, who was always the peacemaker unless her temper was very seriously ruffled.

"She certainly is an even-tempered girl, that Belle Ringold," said Amy, as the two chums moved away. "Mad all the time! Well, Jess, they certainly have put something over on us."

"I think it is a grand idea," rejoined Jessie eagerly. "If it is partly an amateur concert there will be just so many more people interested in it and thereby interested in the hospital foundation fund."

"But, honey! The fact remains," Amy said rather ruefully, "we are not in it!"

"But we are going to be," declared her chum decidedly. "We thought of it first——"

"But maybe they won't let us. It can't all be in the hands of the ladies of the hospital committee. I suppose over at Stratfordtown there will be somebody, Mr. Blair, for instance——"

"We'll see him," said Jessie. "And we'll ask Mark. If Mark feels so friendly toward us we'll give him a chance to show it. I am just determined, Amy Drew, to sing in that concert."

"I would like to recite something," sighed Amy. "You know, Miss Seymour praised me for that after our June entertainment at the high school. I am just as eager to get into it as you are, Jess. But I do hate to go to Mr. Blair—or even to Mark Stratford or his father—and ask him right out."

"I am not afraid to ask for what I want," declared Jessie, who had considerable firmness and good sense. "But I wish we could find Mark's watch to return to him. Then there would be some reason in our asking a favor. Though I don't want him to feel that he has got to pay us for breaking down that aerial."

"He can help us get on the program for just any old reason, for all I care," said Amy. "But how are you going to find his watch, Jess?"

"I don't know. I feel that we ought to make inquiries of those children."

"Little Hen and those others?" Amy cried.

"Yes. Mind you," said Jessie seriously. "I do not want to believe, and I do not believe, that Henrietta knows a thing about the watch. But some of the others—well, the poor things haven't had much bringing up, I suppose."

"More like dragging up," chuckled her friend.

"We'll go over to Dogtown in the morning and I'll try to get Henrietta to tell us if she knows anything about the watch."

Amy Ties a Knot

CHAPTER VII

AMY TIES A KNOT

THE Roselawn chums listened in that evening to a fine concert from one of the more distant sending stations. It did seem, as Amy said, as though it was a good thing that Mark Stratford had plunged with his aeroplane through the aerial and forced the girls to restring it. At least, the sounds from Jessie's receiving set were much clearer than before.

"No atmospherics and little interference from other sending stations," Jessie declared. "Wait. Let me tune in on Stratfordtown. Perhaps they are sending something good, too."

She knew the wave length of the Stratford Electric Company plant, and after adjusting the "cat's whisker" on the detector she moved the tuning slides with care. Into their ears there came gradually a mellow voice singing one of the girls' favorites, a selection from a lesser grand opera.

"Madame Elva!" gasped Amy. "I would know her voice if—if I heard it in my dreams!"

"So it is," breathed Jessie.

But she would not speak again until the selection was finished. Then she said:

"I hope mother and the other ladies get Madame Elva on that hospital program. And if we get on it, too, dear, won't it be great?"

"I should say! Think of being able to say that we sang and recited on the same program with Madame Elva! Oh, my!"

Amy was always enthusiastic about anything she undertook. In the morning she was over at the Norwood house very early and in boating costume. The girls had a canoe on Lake Monenset and they knew pretty well how both to paddle and sail it. When they went down to the boat-landing belonging to the Norwood place a steady breeze ruffled the lake. It was, as Amy declared, "a gorgeous morning."

"Tell you what, Jessie, honey," said the fly-away. "Let's have Bill get out the sail and step the mast for us. It is a fine sailing breeze. We can make Dogtown at a fast clip."

Jessie was pleased with the proposal. They called the gardener's boy and had him bring the leg-o'-mutton sail from the boathouse. The long canoe was rigged to carry two sails; but the girls never used but one. This Bill stepped forward, and while Jessie held the steering paddle, Amy got in amidships to tend sheet.

The canoe moved out from the landing sluggishly. Jessie had to paddle on both sides to push it into the wind. But when the canoe was out of the shelter of the shore, the first swoop of the breeze filled the canvas and almost yanked the sheet out of Amy's hand.

"Who! Old Boreas almost had me that time," cried the gay-hearted girl. "Now we're speeding, Jess!"

Jessie held to the paddle with both hands. She sat so she could see to starboard of the bellying sail, and she did not notice what Amy was doing. She soon began to realize, however, that the breeze was not as steady as she had at first thought and that it was growing momentarily stronger.

The canoe heeled over a little and she counteracted this with the paddle. But the strain grew more intense. Spray began to drift in over them. Monenset Lake was deep at this point. Although both Jessie and her chum could swim, the former thought that she did not want to be plunged into the water at this point, and with her clothes on.

"Perhaps we had better drop the sail, Amy," cried Jessie. "The wind is coming in puffs."

"Oh, let's keep on. The puffs are just right," the other responded. "They are driving us right for Dogtown landing."

"Goodness!" breathed Jessie, half-frightened "But we don't want to be carried ashore there and smash the canoe. Be ready with the sheet, Amy, when we go about."

"Oh—oh—all right!" gasped her chum, suddenly very busy.

There was a moment of silence.

"What are you trying to do?" cried Jessie.

"I—can't unknot it, Jess!" wailed Amy suddenly.

"What *is* the matter?" gasped Jessie, in some excitement. "What can't you do? Look out, Amy! You'll have the canoe over."

"I—can't—unknot it!" shrieked the other girl again.

"The sheet!" cried Jessie. "Don't tell me you have been so foolish as to tie that sheet?"

"All right. I won't tell you. But I have," replied her chum, evidently trying with all her ingenuity to untie the snarl into which she had recklessly allowed the rope to get.

The sheet-rope governed the management of the sail. Knotted to a cleat at Amy's hand when they first got aboard, the strain of the wind-filled sail had now pulled it so tight that the girl's fingers could not manage it at all.

Her brother, Darry, and Burd Alling, his chum, had taught both Jessie and Amy to make certain naval knots which could be slipped easily in an emergency like this. But Amy had forgotten all about that. She had wound the end of the sheet about the cleat and tied a "hard" knot.

"Wish I had a knife!" wailed the careless girl.

"Oh, Jessie! pay off so as to take the strain off the rope. Maybe——"

But just then another burst of wind swooped down upon the canoe. The latter shot ahead, its nose buried in foam, traveling so fast that Jessie was really frightened.

"Wait! Wait till it's quiet," she shouted to Amy.

If she changed the course of the canoe then, or tried to, Jessie realized that the craft would shoot sidewise to the wind and in all probability the boom would swing over and the weight of the canvas would capsize the light craft. It was a ticklish situation.

Amy was still crying out with alarm. Jessie tried to hold the steering paddle firm. And all the time the canoe tore on, through, rather than over, the rising waves. The spray continued to come inboard in sheets. The girls were saturated.

Finally Jessie saw ahead, and very close to them, the decayed float beside the dock at Dogtown, with the several unpainted shacks behind it that made up the village. The cluster of houses seemed to be shooting right toward them.

"Cut it! Cut it! If I could only cut it!" shouted Amy in despair.

"You might as well talk about biting it off," her chum declared, with considerable disdain.

But Amy did not hear this. And there was little time to do anything or hear anything or say anything. Another fierce puff of wind—a veritable squall—swooped down upon the canoe!

Amy shrieked again. Even Jessie lost what little courage remained to her. Driven by the blast, the canoe shot head on into the old float. There was a terrific crash!

Montmorency Shannon

CHAPTER VIII

MONTMORENCY SHANNON

A GREAT wave of the backwash as they struck the float came inboard and wet both girls to their waists. Amy was now crying hysterically, and Jessie could do nothing to any better use.

The canoe was strongly built for a canoe, but such a collision as this was bound to do it much damage, if it did not completely wreck it. It really was wonderful, as Amy afterward said, that the craft was not overturned and the girls thrown into the water.

But providentially the nose of the craft hit a slanting plank of the old float and shot right up out of the water. It saved the canoe from being utterly smashed; but as the bow went up on the float while the stern sank in the water, the girls were thrown screaming together in the submerged end of the canoe.

"Oh! O-ooh! Jess! I'm d-d-d-drowning!" sputtered Amy Drew.

"Keep your mouth closed; then you won't drown," advised her chum practically, and she began to scramble forward.

The spread sail had strained the canoe very badly. Jessie knew that tiptilted as it was, and wet, it was still full of wind and was tearing at the fastenings of the mast and at the tied rope. When she got to the staff stepped forward, she put her shoulder to it, tugged with both hands, and managed to dislodge the mast.

Down it and the sail came with a crash. Leaving the canvas half in the water and half on the float, Jessie scrambled out over the bow of the canoe. Amy, panting, was just behind her.

"If that wasn't just the meanest job that was ever done!" groaned the dark girl. "What a state we are in, Jess!"

"You *would* tie the sheet in a knot when you have been warned a dozen times to keep it in your hand," complained Jessie.

And that was a pretty strong complaint for Jessie Norwood to make. Hers was a very equable temper, and she was always patient with her chum. But this seemed such a perfectly unreasonable happening. It need not have been.

"If our canoe is utterly ruined, Amy, what shall we do?"

"Maybe Darry and Burd can fix it," Amy rejoined, but she did not speak with confidence.

They could see how the thwarts had been strained apart from the framework, and the bow of the canoe was crushed in. It was a dreary sight. Jessie Norwood did not believe Darry Drew and his chum would be able to patch the broken craft. And she did not want her mother to know how it had been broken.

The minute following their abrupt landing was all the time they had then to discuss the accident. Tearing down to the float from the bunch of houses came a shrieking crowd of boys and girls ranging from six to sixteen, the bare brown legs of Henrietta Haney flashing in the van. Henrietta did not wear her silk dress and silk stockings "common."

"Oh, Miss Jessie! Oh, Miss Jessie! Did you come to see me?" demanded the freckled child.

"I guess we did," Jessie Norwood said ruefully staring at the wrecked canoe. "But we did not mean to come just in this way. Our canoe is ruined."

"Maybe it ain't so bad. I'll call Monty Shannon. He's fixing his wireless, but I guess he'll leave it long enough to look at your boat, Miss Jessie."

"Radio?" murmured Jessie.

"To think of these kids down here having a radio set!" said Amy, quite as surprised as her chum.

"Oh, he ain't got the set yet," explained Henrietta, while the other Dogtown children proceeded to examine the canoe minutely. "But he's got a

lot of wire and things, and he is stringing 'em
from his roof to Patsy Dugan's barn. Monty
says he can catch sounds on those wires like you
catch 'em on yours, Miss Jessie."

"H'mm!" murmured Amy.

"Let us go see what Monty Shannon is doing,"
Jessie said suddenly.

"Now, don't you kids take anything away from
Miss Jessie's canoe, nor do any harm here," in-
structed Henrietta, as she started off in the lead
of the two Roselawn girls.

Henrietta, as the chums had seen before, had
a good deal of influence over her companions of
Dogtown. That was why Jessie began to question the child almost at once.

"Honey," she said, "you and your little friends
came up to see Mr. Stratford's wrecked aeroplane
at my house, didn't you?"

"And it wasn't much more of a wreck than your
canoe," said the sharp little thing. "I guess you'll
have to walk back to Roselawn, Miss Jessie, and
you're all wet, too."

Amy laughed, but Jessie said:

"That doesn't trouble me much, Henrietta.
Our skirts will dry. What I wanted to ask you
about is your being up at Roselawn the other evening with your friends. I didn't see you but a
minute. But you had been there some time, hadn't
you?"

"Before that chauffeur came out and chased us? Yes'm, we was."

"Of course you didn't touch anything?"

"What, me?" cried Henrietta. "Sure I touched things. I wanted to see what that flying plane was made of. I never got so near one—not even a smashed one—before. Course I touched it."

"But you didn't pick anything up and carry it away?" Jessie asked earnestly.

"What you meaning, Miss Jessie? Do you think we stole something? That chauffeur did."

"I do not think you stole anything, Henrietta," Jessie assured her. "But something of value has been lost by the young man who fell in the plane. Some of you might have seen it and taken it. And it may still be up there at my house."

"I guess you'd better look again, Miss Jessie," declared the freckled child with her old-fashioned manner. "I know I never touched nothing to bring it away. And I didn't see any of the other kids do it."

"They might not have told you," suggested Amy.

"What? Charlie Foley and the Costello twins and Monty Shannon? Huh! They wouldn't dare try to hide anything from me. Ain't I Spotted Snake, the Witch?" and she laughed elfishly. "They can't hide anything from me."

"Perhaps they hid this from you," Amy observed.

But Jessie said nothing more at the time. They came to the place where Montmorency Shannon and two of the smaller boys were just raising the aerial between the Shannon chimney and the Dugan barn roof. Monty was a rather good-looking boy of fourteen with a shock of rusty hair. His eyes were sharp, and blue, and had a twinkle in them.

Soon after Jessie began to talk with him she discovered that he knew quite as much about radio telephony as she did herself. He had never had a set and he did not own one now.

"But I'm going to get this aerial up. Then I'll be ready for the set—when I can get it."

"But how do you purpose getting it?" Amy asked. "They cost quite a lot of money."

"I know. The set I want costs fifteen dollars," Monty declared. "Maybe it will begin to rain radio sets when I'm ready for mine. I'm going to set out a big tub to catch 'em, if it clouds over."

This amused Amy, but Henrietta thought it was impolite.

"You'd better speak politer than that, Montmorency Shannon, or I'll tell your mother," she declared. "Miss Jessie and Miss Amy have come visiting me. They have to be treated nice."

"All right," laughed the boy. "When I get my radio rigged they can come down here and listen in on it."

Jessie thanked the rusty-haired boy, but she was by no means satisfied. She and Amy went around among the houses, convoyed by Henrietta, and were introduced to several of the housewives that they had not met before. Of course they spent some time with Mrs. Foley, and Jessie asked particularly about Charlie who appeared to have got a job. He was old enough to work. The Rose-lawn girl could not bring herself to the point of discussing the lost watch directly with any of these people. She did not know which child to suspect —if any.

But when she and Amy had bade their acquaintances of Dogtown good-by and were walking up the long lane toward Bonwit Boulevard, Jessie noticed that her chum was very grave.

"Why the seriosity, Amy?" she asked, smiling quizzically.

"Jess, I am puzzled," admitted the other girl.

"So am I. Are you puzzled about the same thing I am?"

"That red-haired boy!" exclaimed Amy vigorously. "He's awfully smart. And he is just as poverty-stricken as the other Dogtown kids, you know he is."

"Well?"

"Then *how* is he going to get a fifteen dollar radio set? I want to ask you! Isn't that a very suspicious thing, Jessie, to your mind?"

"I hate to think the boy is dishonest," confessed her chum slowly. "But, of course, it does look strange. If he *had* picked up the watch, and sold it to some dishonest person, he might have made fifteen dollars. Oh, Amy! it is awful to distrust anybody."

"Humph! Maybe it is. But Mark thinks a lot of that watch and I think we ought to tell him."

"I suppose you are right," agreed Jessie, with a sigh.

Trouble in Prospect

CHAPTER IX

TROUBLE IN PROSPECT

THE two chums did not see Mark Stratford for some days, in spite of the fact that the young aviator came out of his accident so miraculously. They had not been at home when he had called to thank Mrs. Norwood for her kindness, and he was not likely to come especially to Roselawn to call on Jessie and Amy, for both his age and his various interests precluded his desiring the society of girls so young. Amy sometimes said, glumly:

"Darry and his friends think they haven't any time for their 'kid sisters' and their friends. But wait till they want something—a button sewed on, or knicker tapes fixed, or a book found, or something. Then 'little sister' is just as handy to have around as a little red wagon. Humph! What is six or seven years in age, Jess? I ask you."

"Six years of age will make all the difference for us that it has for Darry and Burd—and more," laughed Jessie Norwood. "Don't be wishing your life away, dear."

"I'm not," declared her chum. "I don't want to be any older than I am. I have none of Belle's

aspirations for grown-up-ness, let me tell you.
Only, I have always wished that Darry was
younger than I, so that I could boss him and snub
him and do all those nice things to him that other
girls do who have younger brothers."

"Oh, Amy!" cried Jessie, horrified, for she secretly thought Darrington Drew a wonderful fellow.

"Now, don't 'Oh, Amy!' me, please, honey. I
mean what I say. See how Nell Stanley bosses
Bob and Fred around."

"But she is just the same as a mother to those
boys and to Sally," observed Jessie.

"And to the doctor, too," laughed Amy suddenly. "I'll say Nell rules the whole parsonage."

"She is a very capable girl."

"True. But she can't get very far ahead of
Doctor Stanley. He is the funniest man, Jess! It
is so nice to have a pastor with a sense of humor,
isn't it?"

"Momsy says that the sense of humor is something that all clergymen must have. They have
so much to contend with."

"And I'll say Doctor Stanley has it big," said
Amy, nodding. "I was there the other day to
take a book back to the doctor that papa had borrowed, and while I was in the study Nell was discussing household mechanics with her father."

"Household mechanics?"

"It takes a good mechanic, Nell says, to make both ends meet on the doctor's salary. And this time it was Bob's birthday that came to the fore. What should they have for dinner that would be a treat, you know. Said the doctor:

" 'Bob's birthday? You don't say so, Nellie. How that boy is getting on! But what about it?'

" 'Nothing much, Reverend,' Nell said, 'only I thought we ought to kill those two Rhode Island Red chickens.'

"And then the doctor said, his eyes crinkling up at the corners in that funny way of his:

" 'But, Nellie, how can you blame those two chickens for what happened fourteen years ago?' "

Jessie laughed delightly at this. It was so typical of the good clergyman's humor. But she spoke with gravity, however, when she said:

"There's Nell, too. I know she would like to do something on the program for the hospital fund. She sings awfully well, Amy."

"Say!" exclaimed the eager Amy. "Remember that trio we three sang for the Sunday School Union that time? I know you want to sing your solo; and I want to recite. But if we could take Nell in, too, and make a trio of it— Oh, Jess! Let's ask your mother."

Jessie agreed to this; but when they arrived home they found Mrs. Norwood busy with various affairs connected with the charitable drive and Jessie had to sit down to the telephone and call up one person after another to whom her mother wished to send messages.

"Wish we could broadcast all this," she said. "It certainly will be fine when every family has both a receiver and sender. Why, when that day comes, ordinary telephones will be scarcely necessary."

"I don't know that I would want to send into the air all my private affairs," laughed her mother. "You know, sometimes I talk to Doctor Leffert over the telephone and tell him my symptoms—or the symptoms I think I have. Such very personal affairs——"

"And see!" broke in Amy, eagerly. "The air would be crowded with a lot of folks talking at once. Think of that Sara Truro, down on Breen Street, who chatters just like a magpie. She'd get the air and Central would have to say, 'Busy' to everybody else for hours at a time."

"How very ridiculous," chuckled Jessie. "A million people can talk at once on the ether without interference. Our radio telephones will be tuned to certain lengths of wave. If the person you want to talk to is busy, he shuts you out with a switch and will send you a signal to that effect. Oh, it's coming!"

"So's that radio concert," her chum said, with

a laugh. "Oh, I hope we can get in it, Mrs. Nor-wood."

"Now, don't, my dears, talk to me about that now. And remember it is not all my 'say-so.' We can have only so many amateur numbers. People will open their receiving sets for the professionals like Madame Elva and for the string band that has been arranged for. Mr. Blair himself has prom-ised to make the announcements and Doctor Stan-ley will address the audience from the sending sta-tion on behalf of the hospital's need. Mr. Blair will, too, have the concert announced for a week in advance, both at two and at eight o'clock. We hope that will stir up considerable advance inter-est in our need."

Amy was rather despondent when Jessie was excused from the telephone and the girls were again out of doors.

"I suggested this scheme, didn't I?" she de-manded of her chum. "I said 'radio concert' first. And now look! Maybe we won't get a chance to do stunts at the sending station at all!"

"We'll just go and ask Mr. Blair himself. He seemed rather abrupt; but I think he's nice."

"Or Mark. Why not ask Mark?" said Amy. "He says he wants to make it up to us for smash-ing the aerial."

"If we must ask Mark, we must," agreed Jessie.

"But I'd like to find that watch of his before we ask a favor of him."

The two friends made another thorough search of the vicinity where the aeroplane had crashed. It did not seem as though the watch with the diamond-set case could remain hidden in the soil or the grass or in the upturned sod which marked the scene of the accident.

"I've got a pain in my back bending over and poking around so much," sighed Amy. "It positively is not here. Oh, dear, Jess! It is awful to think it, but I feel that Montmorency Shannon must know something about the watch."

"I don't want to think that," said her friend positively.

"But how could a boy like him get fifteen dollars together to spend for a radio set? And he says he is going to get it."

"Maybe he just dreams he will," Jessie rejoined more lightly. "Anyway, Amy, let's not suggest the idea to anybody else. I don't want to get that red-haired boy in trouble."

"I declare! How about Mark, who is our friend?" Amy cried. "If Monty picked up the watch and sold it——"

"Mark Stratford can much better afford to lose his watch than that Shannon boy can afford to be accused wrongfully of stealing," Jessie said quickly. "I should think you would see that, Amy Drew."

"Oh, well, I suppose you are right," agreed the other girl. "Just the same, if we helped Mark to recover his watch our having important parts on the radio program—or on *some* program— would be all plain sailing. Mark would say: 'Anything I can do for you, girls?' You know how generous he is, anyway. Oh dear! I am afraid there will be heartaches over this concert program."

"Oh! I hope not!" cried Jessie.

"What do you suppose is scheduled on the ether for right now? Come on, if your mother doesn't want your help any longer, and let's listen in," said Amy.

The Roselawn radio girls were at the receiving set in Jessie's room much of the time, both day and evening, when there was nothing else of importance to do. Now, when they opened the switch and put the phones to their ears they ran against a trouble that many an amateur finds and at first does not understand the cause of.

"Why, here!" cried Amy after a minute. "I don't hear good. Do you, Jess? Is there something the matter with my phones?"

"I hear the signals waning, too," returned her chum. "And the sounds started strong. Funny."

"I can hardly hear now. There is something wrong."

"Maybe the battery is running out," Jessie suggested.

"What's that mean?"

"Goodness, Amy! You know that sometimes a doorbell won't ring because the battery has failed."

"But this battery isn't like a doorbell battery, is it?"

"Exactly. It's a B battery. And a B battery is merely a collection of dry cells. The voltage is twenty-two and a half. That is because the detector-tube gives best results when the voltage on the plate of the tube does not exceed that figure. The number of electrons flowing between filament and plate depends on the plate potential up to a certain point——"

"Whatever that is!" ejaculated Amy, stopping her. "Don't be so scientific."

"Not much science about that," laughed her chum. "But our B battery, I fear me, needs renewing. You see, any dry battery recuperates considerably when not in use. These signals sounded loud enough when we first listened in. But the sounds soon decreased."

She took off her earphones. "I'll go and telephone to Mr. Brill to send up a fresh series of batteries for the set. I have no tester, so I do not know how weak these batteries are."

"I remember something," said Amy suddenly. "Once when our doorbell wouldn't ring Darry opened the battery cases and soaked them in vinegar. Wouldn't that work in this case?"

"Nothing like that," cried Jessie, waving her hands. "That might be all right for a doorbell arrangement; but any such rejuvenation around a radio equipment won't do. You'd be breaking down again—and perhaps right in the middle of something you wanted very much to hear."

So she insisted upon running downstairs to telephone to the hardware store in Melford that carried electric appliances. Jessie Norwood had learned a good many practical things about radio telephony and its appliances. This because she had insisted upon erecting her set with only the help of Amy and some small advice from Amy's brother and his chum, Burd Alling.

They heard from the two young collegians that evening. They were at the yacht club moorings to which Darry Drew had brought his yacht, the *Marigold,* again. The yacht was one that Darry's uncle had willed him as a legacy and which he had put into commission for the first time this summer. As yet his sister and Jessie had not even seen the *Marigold.*

"But they will give us a chance to go aboard of her next time they sail," Amy said, when she told Jessie that evening that the boys were on their way home. "That is something else we want to do almost as much as we want to get on a radio program."

"Yes, indeed. I do so want to go aboard that yacht," sighed Jessie. "Why, Amy! I am afraid I am getting covetous, I want so many new things."

Amy chuckled. "Honey," she said wisely, "if we didn't want things, and want 'em bad, the world would stand still. So Father Drew says, and you know he is a very smart lawyer."

The Girls Help Out
Off on the "Water Thrush"

CHAPTER X

THE GIRLS HELP OUT

DARRINGTON DREW and Burd Alling
arrived at Roselawn in the morning, and
as soon as they heard of Mark's accident
they got out the Drew's second car and drove
over to Stratfordtown.

"And they never even suggested our going,"
Amy said, with a pout. "Brothers are so impolite."

"Burd isn't your brother, dear," said Jessie,
laughing.

"But he feels he can treat me just as though he
were. After all, Jess, Mark Stratford is a whole
lot nicer to us. He acts as though we were
grown up."

"You seem to be taking a leaf from Belle
Ringold's book," said her chum scornfully. "I
do not want to be treated as though I were twenty-
five. No, indeed."

"I don't believe even Belle wants to be considered twenty-five," giggled Amy.

When the boys came back from Stratfordtown
they reported Mark as having almost recovered
from his fall in the aeroplane.

"You can't kill that bird with an ax," declared

Alling, in his cheerfully slangy way. "He has been through more trouble than a hen with twenty-four ducklings. He's fallen down from the sky, and been shot out of a car over a cliff, and shot down by Fritzes, and shot up by highwaymen, and——"

"You've a fine imagination," interrupted Amy scornfully. "We saw Mark fall, and he wasn't any better looking when he landed than any other unfortunate victim."

"Say," Darry said, "what do you suppose became of that watch of his?"

Jessie and Amy looked at each other and the former slightly shook her head. So Amy was apparently as unsuspicious as the boys themselves.

"If he came down the way he said he did, a bird might have picked it out of his pocket and he wouldn't know about it," declared Burd. "Huh! Think of bothering your head about a watch when you've just smashed a perfectly good airplane all to bits."

"I guess he thinks more of his grandmother's gift than he did of the plane," said Jessie. "But Amy and I have looked all around and we can't find the watch."

"By the way," demanded Darry, "what's this Mark was telling us about a program to be given out by radio telephony at the Stratfordtown station? He says you girls are running it."

"Oh!" gasped Amy. "I wish we were."

But Jessie saw the twinkle in Darry's eye. "We hope to have a part in it, Darry," she said. "But mother and the other ladies of the hospital fund committee are in charge."

"Gee!" drawled Burd Alling. "Are you two girls really going to do something on a radio program? Then why not Darry and me? Darry could do a clog and I know I could turn handsprings."

At this the girls joined the boys in hilarious laughter. But it was a fact that the two collegians would have been glad to enter into the radio affair to help the charitable cause if there had been anything they could do.

When they came back from a run into New Melford later in the evening Darry and Burd approached the moonlit veranda of the Norwood house in a rather despondent state. At least they appeared despondent.

"What *is* the matter with you two boys?" Amy demanded. "Did you smash the machine, or something?"

"It's something," confessed Burd. "We've been roped, tied, and branded. And it is all Darry's fault."

"Not so!" exclaimed the other youth quickly. "You fell as quick as I did."

"What sort of trouble have you got into?"

Darry's sister asked. "Have we girls got to get you out of it?"

"By gracious; I wish you could," groaned out Darry.

"Tell us the worst," said Jessie. "Out with it."

"It's that Ringold girl," said Darry bitterly.

At that Burd burst into a great shout of laughter and held to his sides while he weaved back and forth on the veranda step. Darry aimed a blow at him that the amused fellow dodged.

"I tell you it is Darry's fault," Burd choked. "Too polite! You know how well he has been brought up."

"Aw, you go fish!" growled out Darry. "You can't escape from that girl once she gets her hooks into you."

"But what is it all about?" Jessie asked composedly. "Have you boys no firmness at all?" she went on mockingly. "Must you become the slave of every girl you meet? I did hope that Amy and I had trained you better."

At that Amy went off in what Burd called a "spasm."

"Tell you what," Darry said hurriedly, "those girls are going to have some sort of a shindig down the lake—at Carter's old place—to-morrow night. The moon is about full. Going in canoes and launches. We couldn't get away from Belle and from Sally Moon till we'd promised to meet 'em down there. Box lunch. You know the kind of a kid time it will be," and Darry's disgust sent his sister and Burd almost into hysterics. The latter declared:

"Don't ring me in on the matter of not getting away from them without a promise. I didn't have the wheel of the car. If I had you'd have seen me duck them in a hurry."

"Yes—you—would!" scoffed Darry. "Anyhow, we're roped. We'll go down there and those girls will get mushy over us. Huh!"

"Huh!" repeated his chum, but still with a twinkle in his eye.

"I like that!" scoffed Amy. " 'Get mushy' over you two fellows! What is your opinion of yourselves, anyway?"

"Oh, come now, Amy, what would you do without 'big brother' to help you out of scrapes?" And Darry grinned at his sister.

"It is a sad case, boys," Jessie admitted. "But perhaps we may be able to help you out."

"You help me out of this thing, Jess Norwood, and I will be your friend for life," Darry declared earnestly.

"Seems to me," put in Amy roguishly, "I have heard a similar promise made before. Aren't we forever helping you boys out of scrapes?"

"You ought to be proud to do it," declared Burd Alling, chuckling.

"Whether we are proud to do it or not," continued Jessie, giggling, "we know our duty."

"Sure! 'You seen your duty and you done it,'" declared the irrepressible Burd.

"I have an idea that may help you, Darry," Jessie continued complacently.

"Shoot!" urged Darry. "Don't keep us on tenterhooks. This is serious, I tell you. Belle Ringold said she'd meet me at Carter's, and she'd have a hatbox of lunch."

"Shoebox," put in Burd sepulchrally. "That's what the Moon said to me."

"At a box party you don't actually have to accept the invitation of the first girl who tells you about it," Jessie said demurely. "You might get out your launch, Darry, and Amy and I will be able to find lunch enough for four people. Besides, we know Burd's capacity and taste——"

"Oh! Oh!" groaned Burd. "A foul blow, that."

"That's a bully good idea," Darry declared. "I'd a whole lot rather have you kids along than Belle Ringold and the Moon girl."

Jessie and Amy looked at each other, and both shook their heads. Secretly Darry's cheerful assumption of the childishness of his sister and his sister's chum hurt the latter's pride more than it did Amy's. But Jessie appeared to accept it quite as Darry's sister did.

"Thanks for them kind words, Sir Galahad," murmured Amy. "Who ever said you were the pink of politeness, Darrington Drew?"

"Oh, well," said Darry carelessly. "You know what I mean."

CHAPTER XI

OFF ON THE "WATER THRUSH"

THAT evening the Norwoods had unexpected company to entertain—three motor cars filled with guests. Aunt Ann, who lived near Riverside Drive, brought the crowd; and although they arrived after dinner, Momsy and Mr. Norwood were rather put to it to amuse the guests.

They were not a card-playing crowd, nor did they care for dancing. Somebody spoke of radio, having noted Jessie's aerial when they drove into the grounds.

"I do wish you had placed your set downstairs here in the drawing-room, as I suggested, Jessie," Mrs. Norwood observed in secret to her daughter. "You see, large and comfortable as your room is, we could not squeeze them into it on this hot night."

"Hold on, Momsy! Wait!" said Jessie eagerly. "I believe I can do something to help you out. There is a fine nine o'clock entertainment to-night from Stratfordtown and another from a New York station at ten. Now wait! Let me call Amy on the telephone."

"But, child, you cannot restring all that wire and replace those things, for just this evening."

"Don't you say a word, Momsy. Leave it to me," cried Jessie gaily, and ran off to call her chum.

Amy came over at once, and for half an hour and more the two girls were very busy. Mr. Norwood had purchased at the time of the church bazaar a loud speaker and horn, as well as a lot of flexible cord. Jessie and Amy reconnected the radio set, strung the cord carefully down the stairway and along the hall and into the big room. They linked up the upstairs set with the loud speaker and horn, and just as conversation was lagging and Mrs. Norwood began to wonder what general topic might interest her visitors, signals from the radio began to be heard.

The visitors gathered from the library and porch, took the chairs the girls had arranged, and for two hours enjoyed to the full the music and recitations broadcasted from the two sending stations mentioned.

"Isn't that a great idea!" said Aunt Ann. "I'm going to have a set put in my place. Jessie, you and Amy come to town and tell me what to buy and how to rig it, and I'll take you to a matinee to pay for it, and afterward to dinner at the nicest restaurant I know of."

"You will have your work cut out for you,

girls," said Momsy, laughing.   But she really was
proud of her daughter's ability.   Daddy Norwood said:

"How are you going to string the aerial on top
of Aunt Ann's house?   You know it is nothing
but a slice of brown stone."

"Why, said Jessie, composedly enough, "we'll
have a loop antenna, instead of long wires like
these I have here.   Of course it can be done,
Aunt Ann."

"And we will come for that matinee and the
dinner," cried Amy eagerly.   "Think, Jess; what
are you going to wear?"

The next day the hospital fund committee arranged the further details of the radio concert
that the Stratford Electric Company had agreed
to broadcast.   The time limit was two hours and
the professional numbers were to be interspersed
with amateur efforts.

"At least, we'll get a place on the same program with Madame Elva," Amy said, but with a
sigh.   "But do you know, Jess, I am just stingy
enough to wish that the committee had not given
so much space to Miss Allister's girls' chorus.
Those songs will take from seventeen to twenty
minutes, the best they can do.   They did at the
school exercises, you know."

"That is true," said Jessie.   "And Momsy says
that she doesn't see how they can give me time

for more than one song, and that a brief one."

"And my recitation takes only four minutes. Oh, dear! That Belle Ringold will crow over us unmercifully. She will think she is the whole show if they let her sing in that chorus."

"Well," admitted Jessie, "she really has a loud voice, you know, Amy."

"You said something," her chum said gruffly. "She can yell loud enough to broadcast from Stratfordtown without any radio-sending machine at all!"

"Why, Amy! Belle hasn't a bad voice, I'm sure."

"Humph! Yes, I know," sniffed Amy. "It's the way she uses it."

Jessie entered heartily into the scheme she had herself suggested by which Darry and Burd were to escape the wiles of Belle and her particular chum, Sally Moon. With the help of Alma, her mother's good-natured cook, Jessie arranged a dainty and tasty lunch for herself and Darry. Amy said she was prepared with a big square hat-box of sandwiches and cake for Burd.

"I bet you eat your share," said the stocky fellow, grinning. "A gnat's table d'hote never would satisfy you, Miss Amy."

Of course, Jessie and Amy had not merely "declared themselves in" on the moonlight box party. It was something that Belle and her clique had been planning for some time and practically everybody had been invited.

The day wore to a soft and lovely evening, and at eight o'clock there were many boats on the lake. Roselawn folk for the most part used a public boathouse not far from the Norwood landing. But Darry Drew kept his *Water Thrush* under a little hut near by. He had been so busy with the *Marigold* since commencement that he had scarcely touched the little launch. But Bill, the Norwoods' gardener's boy, had polished up the engine and kept the launch in good trim.

The quartette found the *Water Thrush* ready for them. Burd staggered down to the landing with the hatbox, apparently scarcely able to bear the weight of the lunch Amy had packed for Burd Alling and herself.

"I'm hungry now," declared the stocky youth, putting down the box carefully. "When do we eat?"

"We don't eat at all till we go ashore at Carter's," said Jessie, with severity. "We heard to-day that somebody had been down there and had swept and garnished the old kitchen."

"I hope they went upstairs and cleared out the snakes," giggled Amy.

"I hope so, too," agreed her chum. There had been an occasion when the Roselawn radio girls had had a rather thrilling experience with some black snakes that had preëmpted the old Carter house. "If those snakes ever came tumbling down into the kitchen while this bunch of girls and fellows were eating, mercy! what a row there would be!"

"I never did know what snakes were for," sighed Amy. "Nature is wonderfully efficient, we know. But why snakes?"

"So that they can make snakeskin purses for you girls to carry. That's easy," declared Burd solemnly.

"That's a good one," laughed Darry, pulling a paper out of his pocket and unfolding it in the light of the binnacle lamp at the stern. "See here. I copied this list of startling explanations that Professor Totten has collected during the course of his long career teaching the youthful idea to shoot. That snake business of yours, Burd, ought to go down to posterity in their company. These are selected, the Profes. says, from many that he has picked out of freshman and sophomore papers. Listen:

"'Joan of Arc was the wife of Noah.'

"'Tobacco was introduced into England by Henry Clay.'

"'Romulus and Remus were a couple of Siamese twins who made Rome howl.'

"'Fratricide is a friend who murders a college student. Insecticide is a man who kills his aunt.'

" 'The Nihilists are the people of the Nile country.'

" 'Sodom and Gomorrah are the two Hebrew children who were burned in the fiery furnace.'

" 'A misanthrope is a man who marries his own wife.'

" 'The treaty of Ghent was so called because every man brought his own drink.' "

"Goodness gracious Agnes!" sputtered his sister. "Do you mean to say that college students don't know any better than *that?* Where do they pick them—out of the infant class?"

"You shouldn't have read these girls that, Darry," complained Burd, when Amy and Jessie had laughed their fill. "They'll lose all respect for our erudition. That will never do!"

"You don't suppose," drawled Amy, "that we are really impressed by your superabundance of knowledge and your wonderful brainery? No, no! We know you too well. Look out, Burd Alling! Don't run us ashore."

"Well put," agreed her brother. "Try to keep your eyes open, old Sleepyhead. We don't want to have to walk back from Carter's."

The young people from New Melford proper all went by bus and automobile to the lower end of Monenset Lake, where there was a landing and a boathouse at which canoes and rowboats could be hired. The lake, shaped like an elon-

gated comma, swept around to this point, passing
Dogtown on one hand and the old and abandoned
Carter estate on the other.

Belle Ringold and her party were nearer the
half demolished dwelling belonging to the old
plantation than were Darry and his party; but
the latter in the *Water Witch* came into view of
the big bonfire on the shore at the Carter place as
soon as the flotilla from the Lower Landing.

The Ringolds were wealthy people, and Belle
could usually do about as she pleased. She had
sent several of her mother's servants ahead and
preparations had been made for dancing on the
smooth yard before the old house, while inside the
long picnic tables were laid for supper.

The moon had come up in wonderful effulgence
and now poured its light over the plaza before the
house. But the bonfire served as a beacon when
the various craft, filled with singing and laughing
picnickers, headed for the shore.

"Is that your boat, Mr. Drew?" shrilled a voice
that could never be mistaken for any but that of
Belle Ringold. "Was so afraid you wouldn't
come."

Darry groaned horribly. Burd, with muffled
laughter, replied:

"Don't know how long we can stay. Something
seems to be the matter here. I think old Darry's
sick. And I never was so hungry in all my life."

"Oh, don't let that worry you," Sally Moon broke in. "I've a nice lunch which you can share, Burd."

"That's fine," said the cruel Burd. "I guess I sha'n't starve. Amy, here, is going to share hers with me too. Always well to be prepared against famine."

The *Water Thrush* was now near enough for the girls from New Melford to see who was in the launch. Belle Ringold gave voice to her disdain as usual:

"For the land's sake! Have Amy and Jess tagged along with you, Mr. Drew? How perfectly horrid!"

The Dogtown Tribe
A Surprise

CHAPTER XII

THE DOGTOWN TRIBE

BURD said, later, with a chuckle, that at this speech Amy sputtered worse than the *Water Thrush* itself. But Jessie pinched her chum's arm and warned her to be still.

"What does it matter, Amy?" she said. "Belle says it because she knows we have the best of the argument. We have deliberately put ourselves up as a target for her sharp tongue. We knew we were doing it, didn't we?"

"All right," grumbled Amy. "But I do hope we will get the best of Belle some time."

"We have now," said her chum.

"Pooh! We are only saving these foolish boys. I hope Darry and Burd will appreciate our efforts," Amy sighed. "But of course they will not."

They went ashore with the rest of the young folks, and Amy and Jessie were at once surrounded by a crowd of girls and boys, showing that, if they were disliked by Belle Ringold and her immediate clique, they were popular with a large circle of friends.

Darry and Burd need not have been so afraid of the occasion being a "kid picnic." There were several young fellows of near their own age; and if most of the girls were of the age of Jessie and Amy they were a bright, fun-loving and companionable lot.

A very good talking machine had been brought from the Ringold house, and the selection of dance records was good. Jessie and Amy introduced Darry and Burd to the nicer girls of the party—those whom the young men did not already know. The Roselawn radio chums particularly aided the collegians in escaping the wiles of Belle and Sally Moon.

That the latter two were angry and disappointed could only be expected; but it was their own fault. Darry and Burd enjoyed themselves dancing with the girls with whom Amy and Jessie were intimate.

Naturally there was bred a little friction. Belle Ringold was not a girl who could complacently endure anything which she considered in the nature of a slight. She was angry with Darry Drew and his chum, but her flashing looks were aimed at Darry's sister and Jessie.

"We know whom to thank for the frost we got," she said angrily to Sally Moon. "That Drew fellow hasn't offered to dance with me but once. And you know, as well as I do, Sally Moon, that it was I who first invited him to this box party. Say! Where did those ragamuffins come from? Who invited them to this party, I'd like to know?"

"Why," drawled Sally, her closest friend, "those are some of that Dogtown tribe."

"They must be friends of Jess Norwood. I understand she invites them to her house and her mother lets them stay to dinner," was Belle's scornful observation.

Jessie did not chance to hear these remarks; she was dancing with Darry Drew at the time and that fact was what made Belle Ringold so angry. But Jessie caught sight of Henrietta and several of her little friends standing at the edge of the wood that fringed the old Carter lawns.

She, too, asked: "How did they get here?"

"Who?" the college youth asked. "Oh! Is that little Hen?"

"It most certainly is. Come, please, Darry; I want to speak to her."

"Hullo!" exclaimed Darry under his breath; "somebody else is going to say something to the little Dogtownites, if I'm not mistaken."

He had seen Belle and Sally Moon, who had been dancing together because there was a short-age of male partners, approaching the group of spectators. But Jessie did not pay Belle and the other girl any attention.

"Oh, Henrietta!" she cried. "How did you get over here from your house?"

"Charlie Foley and Montmorency Shannon fixed up your canoe like you said they could, and we paddled across. Gee! Ain't that dance music fine? I'm going to learn to dance some day. Bertha says I shall. *She* dances."

Just then Belle broke in angrily: "I suppose these are some of your friends, Jess Norwood. But if you invited them here I want to tell you and them, too, that I got up this party and I don't want the offscourings of Dogtown here. You can send 'em away, Jess Norwood."

At that Jessie fired up, meek as her spirit usually was.

"I shall do nothing of the kind," she said sharply, as Henrietta and her friends drew away. "Don't go, Henrietta—and the rest of you children. She does not own this place. You have quite as much right here as we have."

"I—want—to—know!" sputtered Belle.

"It is the truth. You children can stay and look on. And at supper time I think we have brought enough lunch for you all to have a bite." She turned her back on Belle Ringold and spoke to the other boys and girls with Henrietta: "Is that you, Monty Shannon? Have you got your radio fixed yet?"

"Got the antenna all strung. Just waiting for

the set now. I've sent for it," said the young radio enthusiast with promptness.

"Oh!" said Jessie, thoughtfully. "Then you've bought and paid for it?"

"Well, I've bought it. I don't pay for it till they deliver it. Oh, I'm going to have it all right."

"Come on," said Darry, breaking in. "There's the encore of that dance. Let's finish it, Jess. See you later, Hen," and he whirled the Roselawn girl away.

Jessie waved her hand at the little group of Dogtown children. Her warm speech had defended Henrietta and her friends from the unpleasant tongue of Belle Ringold. Perhaps the latter might really have succeeded in driving the Dogtown children away; while in the music and dancing of the New Melford and Roselawn young folks, Henrietta and her party took pleasure.

"Isn't it kind of pitiful," Jessie ventured before the dance concluded, "that those children should have to take their pleasure by proxy?"

"My goodness!" gasped Darry, "you're a funny girl, Jess. Do you want to give Hen and those others dancing lessons?" and he chuckled.

"Well, why not?" she asked pluckily. "We like dancing. Why shouldn't they like it in Dogtown just as much?"

"Unanswerable, I'll say!" Darry rejoined, but

smiling broadly. "I believe you were born to be a 'Miss Fixit' for all mankind. You'll go in for settlement work and all that when you get through school."

"Nothing of the kind!" Jessie cried, in some heat. She did not like to have Darry poke fun at her. Somehow that hurt. "But I'd be ashamed if I did not want little children like Henrietta to have a good time, and have it while they are young enough to enjoy it."

"Hullo!" exclaimed the college youth. "You'll stand well in 'psyche' when you become a co-ed, Jess. I can see that."

At that Jessie laughed again. She did not think she was interested in psychology at all; but she knew she was very much interested in Henrietta and her little friends. Especially was she anxious to learn all about Montmorency Shannon's radio set.

"He's going to get it, he says," she whispered to Amy when they next were together. "Says he's ordered it from the factory. Montmorency and his radio set, I mean."

"Oh!" said Amy. "Whom is he buying it from? Do you know?"

"Let's ask him," said Jessie. "I do want to know just how he is going to pay for it. Think! Fifteen dollars is a lot of money for those Shannons. Why, Monty's jacket is in rags."

Amy began to giggle. "Radio is certainly becoming more important than jackets and shoes."

But Jessie sighed worriedly. "I do wish we knew about Mark's watch and what became of it. I hate to suspect those children."

Belle Ringold and her friend let Henrietta's party alone for the time being. Belle seemed to wish to behave before Darry and Burd in a more ladylike manner than was her usual custom.

But it was difficult for her to quell her dislike of the Dogtown "tribe" when Jessie and Amy ushered the children into the great farmhouse kitchen at supper time and placed Henrietta and her friends at one end of a long table, making them members of her own party. There was much merriment at that end of the table, too, for Darry and Burd, as well as others of the radio girls' friends, cheerfully entered into the spirit of the occasion.

"Lucky you brought this hatbox full of good things, Amy," Burd said. "I can see right now that we are going to be able to get outside the whole of it. Let's see if we can fill up these kids. I believe they are hollow all the way down."

"Mrs. Foley says I am," said Henrietta, complacently. "It takes as much to fill me up as it does a lots bigger girl. Bertha can't eat as much as me."

"Where is Bertha?" Jessie asked.

"She's gone to Stratfordtown to work for a lady. And if the lady likes little girls I'm going to live with her too. Bertha says so."

Just about then the crowd had all become seated and the various boxes were opened. A little quietness fell for a moment. Instantly they heard overhead a strange tapping and scratching sound. The loft over the kitchen was supposed to be empty.

"Oh! Do you hear that?" gasped Amy, staring at Jessie Norwood.

"Who is up there, do you suppose?" demanded one of the other girls.

"'Tisn't *who;* it's *what,*" declared Burd Alling.

"What do you mean, Burd?" Sally Moon demanded from the other end of the table.

"There is nobody missing," explained Burd. So——"

Just then little Henrietta offered her contribution to the discussion. She gulped her first mouthful of sandwich and declared hoarsely:

"Snakes!"

"O-o!" shrieked several of the girls.

"Snakes, indeed!" gasped Belle Ringold. "You horrid little thing! How would snakes come to be upstairs in this house?"

"They was here," said Henrietta with confidence, looking at Jessie and Amy. "You 'mem-

ber 'em, don't you, Miss Jessie? They was Carter's ha'nt, wasn't they?"

"There used to be a ghost here, everybody
said," called out some one in the crowd. "Do you
suppose it is a ghost up there?"

Just then the scratching on the floor was repeated. Something not at all ghostly, it seemed,
was moving about in the garret of the old house.

CHAPTER XIII

A SURPRISE

BELLE RINGOLD, who was really nervous over the noise, forgot for the moment her feud with the Roselawn girls. She cried:

"Jess Norwood! do you mean to say you knew snakes were here in this house?"

"Henrietta killed two here," said Jessie, looking at the closed door of the stairway. "But if there are others up there they can't get down while the door is shut."

"I don't believe it!" scoffed Sally Moon. "Somebody is trying to scare us."

"Anyhow," drawled Amy, "it probably isn't a ghost."

Her brother laughed aloud. "If it is," he said, "it must be the ghost of an old hen. Sounds like a hen scratching on a barn floor."

"Something with long toenails anyway," declared Burd seriously. "You can hear 'em."

"Would you say, Burd, that it sounded to you like a bear, for instance?" his college friend said with equal gravity.

"Now, boys, hush!" cried Amy. "We are not

to be scared. Jess and I *were* worried that time by the snakes. But we saw them——"

"And nobody has seen these mysterious critters," put in Chip Truro, who was of the party. "I shut that door when we came in here to fix the tables. Listen! I believe they are hopping down the stairs."

"Perhaps they *are* snakes!" shrieked Amy, jumping up from her seat.

"Don't sound like those others did," said Henrietta, who had kept on steadily eating, and now spoke between swallows. "Them black snakes was fighting before."

"Maybe they have patched up a truce," said Darry Drew. "I tell you it is a chicken."

"It may be a crysomela bypunktater," remarked Burd recklessly. "Does that fact keep me from having another sandwich, Amy?"

"It ought to," said Amy, while Henrietta's eyes opened so wide when she heard Burd's make-believe Latin that she could scarcely bite her own sandwich.

"My!" Henrietta whispered to Jessie. "What lots of things they learn you at them colleges, don't they?"

"There is more than one thing hopping down those stairs," declared Chip. "I reckon it must be a whole flock of those 'bypunktaters' you mentioned, Alling."

"I'm going to find out what it means," declared Sally, who was of a defiant nature. She hopped up and made for the stairway door. "Somebody is trying to play a joke on us."

"Don't do it! Don't do it!" urged Amy. "You don't know, Sally. It might be snakes."

"Snakes with claws on them?" scoffed Sally.

She grabbed the handle of the door. All was silent behind the panels at that moment. A big headlight lantern had been brought along, and this stood upon the old chimney mantel, lighting the whole room. The blazing ray of it was aimed right at the stairway door.

Everybody stopped eating to look at Sally. That is, everybody but Henrietta. The freckle-faced girl was so absorbed in the good things Jessie and Amy had heaped on her wooden plate that she gave small attention to anything else.

"Here goes!" cried Sally Moon.

She jerked open the door. The blaze of lamplight revealed all the stairway landing. There was a black-and-white striped, bushy-tailed creature and several small replicas of the larger one on the stairs. The lamplight evidently dazzled them. They blinked and made no sound.

"For the land's sake!" shouted Belle Ringold, and started up in haste.

"Why, it's a cat and a bunch of kittens," said Sally.

But most of the older members of the crowd, as well as all the Dogtown children, made hastily for the exit of the kitchen.

"Mephitis mephitica!" Darry sang out. "Beat it, folks!"

"What *does* he mean?" gasped Sally Moon, falling back from the door.

The general although unexplained desire of everybody to get away from the vicinity of the stairway amazed Sally, but it startled her too. The group of little animals on the loft stairs seemed the most harmless things in the world.

Suddenly Henrietta came to sudden action. She dropped the cake she had begun on and rushed for the stairway. Sally screamed and fell back out of the freckled little girl's way. Amy screamed to Henrietta to return. But the latter reached the door, grabbed the handle, and slammed it shut again before what Darry had called "Mephitis mephitica" could emerge. At the same time she explained to the bewildered Sally:

"They's skunks, lady."

"Good kid!" shouted Burd Alling. "You certainly take the strawberry tart."

"Have you got any?" asked the practical Henrietta. "I didn't taste any of that yet."

This caused more than a little hilarity among the picnic groups; but like Sally and Belle and their friends, the crowd from Roselawn voted to remove to the out-of-doors to finish supper. The moonlight was sufficiently bright for all purposes, and the near presence of the pariah of the woods and her family made them all "feel creepy," as Amy expressed it.

"This old Carter place certainly offers some startling experiences," Jessie said. "It is nice to come to, but snakes and—an—well, whatever Darry calls them, seem to fancy the place, too."

"Next time we come picnicking I'll send some of the men ahead with a dog and drive out all the wild animals," declared Belle.

"If your dog ever ran into those kitties on the stairway there, he would be the wilder animal," Chip Truro said, laughing. "But they are perfectly harmless if you don't disturb them."

"I hope they won't object to music and dancing," Sally Moon said. "I am going to start the machine again."

"If we only had a radio set here, we could get the ten o'clock entertainment from Stratfordtown," Amy suddenly suggested.

"Why couldn't we, next time we come?" Belle said, catching at the new suggestion instantly.

"You don't rig a radio outfit as simple as all that, do you?" Sally asked.

"You might bring your antenna rigged as a loop," Jessie said quietly. "It would not take long to make the necessary connections."

"Is that so?" Sally observed.

Belle broke in suddenly and called Sally Moon away. She was very eager, and the two friends held a long and private conversation. Amy and Jessie were not usually interested in the personal affairs of Belle and her chum, but it struck the Roselawn radio girls that Amy's remark must have given Belle a new idea. They were to learn more about this later.

The renewal of the dancing gained the attention of all the party, and for an hour more the moonlit space before the Carter house continued a gay scene. Then it was eleven o'clock and Darry's party, at least, thought it time to go home.

Jessie insisted that Henrietta and her party go back to Dogtown, too. The canoe which had been partly wrecked by Amy's misfortune had been repaired very neatly by the oldest Foley boy and Monty Shannon.

"Really," Amy said to her chum, "that Shannon boy is a smart little fellow. It's too bad——"

"Hush! Don't let's say it," whispered Jessie.

"I don't know that we ought to try to hide it, if he did take that watch," grumbled Amy.

"Oh, I hope he didn't!" said Jessie gravely.

"I asked him where he was buying his radio set. He said of the Stratford Electric Company," Amy laughed. "If he sold Mark's watch to get money to buy a radio set, the Stratfords will get fifteen dollars back, anyway."

"How you talk!" exclaimed Jessie. "That beautiful watch is worth several hundred dollars. Whoever bought the watch—if Monty sold it— knows of course that it is valuable and that no boy in Dogtown could rightfully own such a thing. Dear me! I do wish I knew what to do about it."

"How about taking legal advice?" suggested Amy roguishly, for both their fathers were lawers.

"I am afraid to do that," confessed Jessie. "As I said before, to arouse suspicion against Monty Shannon would be a very cruel thing to do if it turned out afterward that he was innocent. No, Amy, I couldn't even tell Daddy Norwood."

A Rather Wet Time

CHAPTER XIV

A RATHER WET TIME

THE young folks who had spent the evening at the old Carter place all got away at about the same time. But once out on the lake, they scattered. By far the larger number of boats were going down the lake to the landing nearer New Melford. The Roselawn crowd headed for the Norwood landing were not sorry for this, for they sooner escaped the sharp tongue of Belle Ringold.

The moon was fast disappearing beyond the wooded hills and a haze was being drawn over the sky. Darry Drew wisely suggested heading immediately for the upper end of the lake and home.

"It will be as dark as a stack of black cats in half an hour, girls. And there's a wind coming up."

"Heavy weather in the offing—aye, aye, Skipper," growled out Burd. "We deep water sailors of the *Marigold* cannot be mistaken in weather changes."

"See how reckless those kids are!" exclaimed Amy suddenly. "They will have that canoe over."

She referred to the Dogtown children. Jessie had been watching Charlie Foley and Montmorency Shannon paddling. Now she urged:

"Can't we keep near them until they get to the Dogtown landing, Darry? If they should be swamped!"

"Never do to let little Hen drown," agreed Darry, chuckling. "She is some kid, I'll say! Maybe we would better tow them to Dogtown."

But the smaller boys would not hear to that when it was suggested. Henrietta declared:

"If they tip us over, or anything like that, Mrs. Foley will fix 'em, Miss Jessie. She told Charlie to look out for us when we started. And, then, Spotted Snake, the witch, will bring 'em bad luck if the boys don't behave good," and she laughed eerily.

Nevertheless, because of Jessie's insistence, the launch followed behind the canoe until the landing was in sight. Therefore the quartette of friends from Roselawn became separated from the other boats headed in the direction of Bonwit Boulevard.

"O-oo!" cried Amy suddenly. "It's getting dark." Then she began to sing the old song about being "Afraid to go Home in the Dark" and Burd came in with what Darry called a shaky second part.

"Nothing out here will ever trouble us with you

two singing that way," he observed.   "You'd
scare the loons."

"Better light your lantern, Darry, hadn't you?"
Amy broke off to ask.

"I don't think anybody will run into us," her
brother said.   "But I hope every other kind of
craft on the lake carries a light."   Nevertheless,
he followed his sister's advice and lighted his
lantern.

The moon had dropped out of sight.   The sky
had grown thick with mist so that not a star
sparkled.   There was a certain glimmer of light
shimmering upon the surface of the water, but
this illumination was not sufficient to exhibit more
than the faintest outlines of objects at their level.

"Go easy, Darry," advised Burd, in a low voice
from the bow.   "I declare I can't see as far as I
can reach."

"You know that is a wood ahead," said Amy.
"It's Jocklin Point.   When we get around that we
shall have a clear way to our landing.   Do you
hear the other folks, Jessie?"

All Jessie could hear was the chugging of the
launch.   The *Water Thrush* was not a fast boat,
but it was seaworthy and roomy.   The Roselawn
young people had enjoyed many pleasant parties
in it.   And Darry was so good a mechanician
that their parents never worried when the young
folks were out on the lake in the *Water Thrush*.

With the moon gone the towering trees on shore cast a perfectly black shadow upon the lake out from Jocklin Point. Soon they could see the clearway beyond the shadow, and Darry increased their speed.

"It's getting close to midnight. We must get home," he said. "Anything in the way, Burd?"

His chum turned his head to look back into the lighted cockpit. "Plenty of water," he began, and just then the launch ran, with a crash, head on upon something.

"What is it? Oh, what is it?" shrieked Amy.

"Oh, Darry!" gasped her chum, and for an instant she seized Darry's arm.

"Now what have you done, you big chump?" demanded the latter of Burd Alling. "You've run us into the shore."

"I haven't been steering the old tub," growled out Burd. "I told you I couldn't see."

"I believe you. You must be stone blind——"

"Oh! Oh!" cried Amy again. "My feet are wet. It—it's sinking!"

"Don't be foolish, Amy," begged her brother. "Squealing won't help us."

"Well, just the same, I'm not going to stay down there and get wet," and she clambered upon the decked-over portion of the launch.

"We never hit the shore, Darry," declared Burd, from up forward.

"What is it, then?"

"She *is* sinking!" interrupted Amy, a second time. "Darry Drew, if you have brought us out here on this lake to drown us, papa and mamma will never forgive you!"

Jessie began to giggle nervously at this. But she scrambled up on the deck-house after her chum. The water was running fast into the bottom of the launch.

Something loomed up beside the shaking boat. Darry sprang to the rail and leaned over to examine the black object.

"A log!" he cried. "No wonder she's leaking. Bet we started every seam in her bow."

"Never mind talking about it," Burd advised. "Get on. If we don't reach the landing——"

"O-ooh! We're going down!" shrieked Amy.

The launch did give a sudden cant to starboard. When it righted, the standing room was knee deep in water. Darry tried to start the motor again and could not. It was fouled, and they were actually helpless.

"There's a boathook, Burd!" Darry cried. "Grab it and hook on to that log."

"That log has done us harm enough already," complained his sister. "Let it go. Oh!"

"Stop your squealing, Amy!" commanded her brother. "You girls get ready to crawl over on that log."

"On the log?" cried Jessie in wonder.

"One thing sure, that log won't sink," said Darry confidently. "But the old *Water Thrush* is on her way. Anything you want in the cabin, girls?"

"There isn't a bite of lunch left," declared the irrepressible Amy. "What Burd didn't eat, little Hen did. Oh!"

"Step over there, girls!" ordered Darry.

He and Burd held the side of the launch close to the rough, wet bark of the big log. It was with some trepidation that Jessie stepped from the dipping rail to the top of the log. Amy shrank from the attempt, for she saw her chum suddenly fall on her knees and almost dive into the black water beyond her refuge.

"Oh! We'll all be drowned!" Amy cried.

"Don't be a dunce, Sis," begged her brother. "If Jess can do it, you can. Be a sport."

"Nev—never let—it—be said that I wasn't a sport!" gasped Amy. "Here I come, Jess!"

The launch was down so low that the water began to slip over the rail into the cockpit. Darry went forward and dropped over the anchor. Burd began to snicker.

"What's the matter with you?" his chum demanded.

"Oh, my eye!" gasped Burd Alling. "Dropping the anchor! Believe me, boy, this launch will be right here—on the bottom—without any iron down. Woof! Here we go!"

He leaped for the log, missed it by half a foot, and splashed into the water with a frightened cry.

At this Amy gave forth a yell that, one might have thought, could be heard from one end of the lake to the other. Jessie clutched the log tighter and gasped. Darry grabbed the boathook and caught the hook into the waistband of his chum's trousers as he went down.

Sputtering and shouting, Burd was drawn to the surface again. The girls added their screams to the young fellow's objections. Darry leaped to the log and managed to keep his chum above the surface. The latter, between his sputtering and objections to such rough treatment, scrambled up the rough bark and finally hung over the log, panting.

"Why—why didn't you let me alone?" he managed finally to gasp out. "I can swim."

"Couldn't take chances of losing you, Burd," giggled Amy.

"Oh!" cried Jessie. "The launch has sunk!"

She spoke truly. The battered boat had disappeared beneath the surface of the lake. The log rolled slightly. The girls both squealed again, for they were now astride the log and their feet dipped into the lake.

"Oh, dear me!" groaned Jēssie Norwood. "This is an awfully wet time. How shall we ever get home, Darry?"

"Well, there is one thing sure," declared Amy's brother in deep disgust. "We shan't wade ashore. For right about where we are now Lake Monenset is, they say, a quarter of a mile deep."

Not So 'Much Fun

CHAPTER XV

NOT SO MUCH FUN

THE danger, Jessie had thought, was over. But what Darry Drew said made her feel anxious again.

"You don't suppose we shall have to stay here until daylight, do you?" she demanded.

"Too bad we haven't your radio—or some radio—Jessie," said Amy. "If we could send out a cry for help——"

"Hey!" grumbled Burd Alling. "You'll have to send out any wireless like that with your lungs. Come on! Let's all shout. Maybe somebody on shore will hear us."

"Maybe we can make the folks in the other boats hear," Jessie suggested.

They lifted their voices in unison and shouted. Again and again the cry for help ricochetted across the water. But not a sound was returned. There had been so much singing and laughing and shouting on the lake this evening that none of the dwellers along shore would suspect that there was a party in need of rescue.

"You don't suppose the far end of this log is fastened to the shore, do you, Burd?" suggested Darry.

"Not much. I can see the trees now. We're forty yards or more out, I bet. And this log is drifting out into the lake all the time."

"That's what I thought," agreed the older fellow.

"We might swim it," Burd said.

"But Jocklin Point is an awfully lonely place. We'd never get through that tangle of woods," said Jessie quickly.

"Guess you are right, there," Darry agreed, hopelessly.

"And I can't swim so very good," Amy confessed. "I—I'm afraid to try it. In the dark, too."

"Looks as if we'd have to stay here and drift about until morning," Burd said in disgust. "Wish we'd saved some of the lunch."

"How can you speak of such things when you are in danger of drowning?" moaned Amy. "It—it isn't reverent."

"Wow!" yelled Burd. "I felt a snapping turtle at my toe."

"You did not! You did not!" cried the excited Amy. "You just say that, Burd Alling, to frighten me."

But she cocked her feet up on the top of the

log and from that time on was in danger of toppling off.

"We can keep you afloat, Sis," her brother declared. "Guess we'd better push for the shore."

"Not at the point," Jessie objected. "We'd never be able to land there. And the mosquitoes would eat us up. There's a regular swamp."

"Then, how about crossing the lake?"

"I won't! I won't!" repeated Amy, with decision.

"We'll leave her here and swim ashore and get a boat," suggested the wicked Burd.

"You dare!" cried Amy. "Now you've got me all worked up. I—I won't be able to sleep all night."

At that the others burst into laughter, in which Amy joined.

"You sure won't sleep here on this log," said her brother. "That's a cinch. Come on, Sis; brace up. We are in no immediate danger——"

And just then the log rolled and the girls screamed again. Amy sputtered some more.

"I'm wet to my knees! My slippers are ruined! Isn't this awful, Jess Norwood?"

"It is not half as bad as though turtles *were* nibbling at our toes," said her chum.

"Oh!"

"One of the boys might swim ashore for help," pursued Jessie.

"Guess we'll have to come to it," Darry admitted. "Jess has got the right idea."

"But suppose he gets cramp?"

"You're proving the possession of a fine imagination," said Burd. "All right, Darry. Who will be the sacrifice—you or I?"

"Wait a moment!" cried Jessie suddenly. "I hear something."

They held their breath and listened. Amy was about to let loose a flood of questions, when the sound that had caught her chum's attention was repeated.

"I hear it!" Amy cried.

"What is it?" demanded Burd.

Jessie pitched her voice high and sang out:
"This way! This way! We're wrecked!"

"Is it really somebody shouting?" asked Darry.

Again they heard the call. It seemed to come from the other side of the lake—the shore where the Dogtown boat landing was situated.

"Again! All together!" ordered Burd Alling.

At that the shipwrecked party raised their voices once more and made the echoes ring. Their cries startled birds in the trees along the shore and some of them made angry protest. A pair of horned owls swept out of a grove and went "hoot-hooing" through the bottoms, to the terror of field mice and other small game.

Amy shuddered, too, when it was over. "Those

birds always give me the shakes," she gasped. "Was it them shouting, do you suppose?"

But now the cry, and an unmistakably human cry, came nearer. There was a craft approaching. Darry stood up cautiously, balancing himself on the log, and gazed over the murky lake.

"I see it! It's coming!" he muttered.

Then an eery cry reached their ears. Jessie gasped.

"It's that child!" she cried.

"What child do you mean?" demanded Darry.

"Little Henrietta. That is who it is." She raised her voice again and cried: "Henrietta! We're here!"

"Comin', Miss Jessie!" responded "Spotted Snake, the Witch," and a chorus of boys' voices joined hers in encouragement.

The mended canoe soon came into view. Little Henrietta was in the bow.

"I knew it! I knew it!" she cried eagerly. "I seen your light go out from the dock, so I knowed you have been sunk. Then you yelled, and the boys said they'd come out and see."

But the canoe could only take in two of the castaways at a time. The girls went first, and when they had landed with Henrietta at Dogtown, Charlie Foley and Montmorency Shannon went back to the log to rescue Darry and Burd.

The two collegians did not let the boys do this

for nothing; and all of them praised Henrietta until she ran away. The mishap had ended without serious disaster; but Amy complained a great deal walking home to Roselawn.

"Next time I go out with you fellows in a boat, you'll know it," she said. "And I got wet, and lost my sweater, and now it will be two o'clock when we get home."

"Lucky we aren't out there for all night," said her brother. "Don't be a grouch, Sis."

But Jessie loudly praised Henrietta and "the Dogtown kids." Particularly did she praise Monty Shannon. Amy squeezed her chum's arm. She knew why Jessie spoke so warmly of the red-haired boy.

Not too much was made at home of the adventure. But Darry and his chum, with the help of some of the men servants, had a hard job during the next two days raising the *Water Thrush*. Therefore Jessie Norwood and Amy Drew were obliged to find entertainment without the assistance of the young collegians.

CHAPTER XVI

THE REHEARSAL

WHILE the girls of Roselawn and their friends found a dozen vacation activities to interest them, the hospital fund committee did not mark time. Mrs. Norwood was away from home almost every afternoon attending meetings and arranging for talent for the great radio concert. Her mother's absence put upon Jessie's mind certain responsibilities relating to the household that she usually did not have.

But Jessie was a born housewife. Flyaway Amy knew very little about such things, and she admitted that she dodged all responsibilities of the kind when she could. She preferred to sit on the Norwood porch and knit or read or chat with other girls gathered there while her chum busied herself with these extra duties.

Whenever Jessie was at the radio set, however, Amy was on the spot. During these weeks since first the receiving set had been established in Jessie's sitting room, the chums had learned a great deal about radio telephony.

"And according to these books and magazines,

Jess," Amy said, "there is going to be something
new to learn every day. I don't see but we shall
have to give up almost everything else, if we expect to keep up to date in this science."

"I suppose there's bound to be new wrinkles to
learn all the time," admitted Jessie. "But we
have got a lot of information about the receiving end of the business. What I am anxious to
learn is more about the other end."

"The sending end?" asked Amy.

"Yes. We did not see much of it that time
Mark took us up to the Stratford Company's
sending station, where we met Mr. Blair."

"Say, Jess!" Amy said suddenly. "Isn't that
funny?"

"Maybe it is. Only I don't know what you
mean," said her chum, wonderingly.

"That Superintendent Blair's name should be
the same as Hen's cousin?"

"What are you saying, Amy?" demanded Jessie
in amazement. "Why, Henrietta's cousin's name
is Bertha——"

"Bertha Blair—yes!" Then Amy giggled. "I
mean his last name. Blair."

"Well, that has nothing to do with our knowledge of the sending end of radio telephony," said
Jessie, with some impatience. "We saw the
soundproof rooms, and the heavy curtains they
draw about the glass walls to deaden all exterior

noises, and the transmitter horns into which the performers spoke or sang. But a lot of it I didn't understand."

"Neither did I understand it," confessed her friend.

"I have been reading up on that one at Strat-fordtown. It really is a wonderfully powerful transmission set. Think of it! A five hundred watt, three to six hundred meter broadcasting set. And with it they use an amplifier that magnifies the voice a hundred thousand times—and that without producing any distortion."

"Humph!" grumbled Amy. "Then when Belle Ringold sings with that chorus it isn't going to sound much worse than usual, is it?"

"Don't talk that way. She and Sally are mad enough at us because of the other night," said Jessie.

"My telling you what I think of the quality of her singing voice isn't going to make Belle any madder," chuckled Amy. "But Darry says she won't speak to him now—nor to Burd Alling. Of course, they are terribly unhappy about it," grinned Amy.

"Sally and Belle are awfully busy about something," Jessie said reflectively. "Nell Stanley told me that there is something new afoot. Mrs. Ringold was offended the other day at the meeting of the hospital committee. She came to Doctor Stanley with a long tale of woe. But you know how the doctor is. Nell said he refused to take sides. The hospital is something bigger than a church interest, and he told Belle's mother so."

"I hope she isn't planning to do anything to hurt the hospital concert," said Amy quickly.

"Oh, I don't know that she would do that; but she is a good deal like Belle—a trouble maker."

"We certainly have found that out about her daughter," laughed Amy. "And when is the crowd to go over to Stratfordtown to rehearse?"

"In the morning. Miss Allister has had a lot of trouble with the chorus. That's another stir-up," sighed Jessie.

"They need not worry about me," said Amy with conviction. "I am letter perfect in my recitation. I'm not scared a bit. When I stand up before the audience— Oh, honey! There will not be any audience, will there?" and she ended with a laugh.

"Not much of one, I guess," said Jessie. "It must be like playing in the movies. There is no inspiration of applause. But I expect for the rehearsal to-morrow half the people who own motor-cars in New Melford and Roselawn will sail over to Stratfordtown. It will look like circus day over there."

"Jess, you hit it right," her chum said, when the Norwoods' big car, driven by Chapman, was

parked in one of the lanes beside the Electric
Company's stockade at ten o'clock the next fore-
noon. "It does seem as though there must be a
street fair in the town, or something of the kind."

The radio girls of Roselawn had been up to the
sending station on a previous occasion, so they
could take "Momsy" right along with them. They
knew the location of the elevators. Neither Mark
nor his father was present, but Mr. Blair, the
radio superintendent, remembered the chums and
addressed them as they stepped out of the elevator
with Mrs. Norwood.

"Just a moment and I will be with you, young
ladies," he said, in his rather brusk way.

He was talking with a girl whose back was
toward the newcomers; but when the latter
had moved away from the elevator Amy suddenly squeezed her chum's arm to draw her
attention.

"Isn't that Bertha, little Hen's cousin?" asked
Amy in a whisper.

"Of course it is," said Jessie, gladly. "Wait!
I'll get a chance to speak with her."

"Do you suppose she is trying to get on the
program, too?" asked Amy, in surprise.

"It may be. They pay a small fee I believe to
those who really are able to render an interesting
number. Didn't little Henrietta say that Bertha
could sing?"

"Of course she did. There! Will you speak to Bertha?"

Jessie was ready to do just that. She saw Mr. Blair turn from the plainly dressed girl with some hesitancy. As though his gaze was held against his will the superintendent stood looking after her.

"Why, Bertha!" Jessie exclaimed, meeting Henrietta's cousin with outstretched hand. "How glad I am to see you again. Father would like to see you, too. Especially if you find yourself in need at all," and she smiled at the girl.

"Oh! Is it you, Miss Jessie? I have a place in Stratfordtown here. But they told me that I might earn a little extra here evenings by singing. And I would like to make enough to have little Henrietta with me."

"Why, I know Daddy Norwood feels so grateful to you for helping him in the Ellison case that he would gladly do something for you and Henrietta. We have already talked about it."

"But I could not take anything in payment for telling the truth in court," declared the other girl hastily. "You know, that would not be right."

"We-ell," said Jessie hesitatingly. "Perhaps not. I am afraid you are a wee bit proud, Bertha."

"Yes, ma'am," said Bertha. "I was taught pretty good. My father came of good folks, and mother's people were nice, if they were poor. Mrs. Foley tells me I've a lot of folderols in my head where my brains ought to be," and she laughed gently.

"Did you get the chance to sing, Bertha?" asked Jessie suddenly.

"Not just now, the gentleman said. But he said I might come again and he would try me out at rehearsal."

She turned away with a bright smile and nod. But Jessie asked another question:

"Did you tell him your name, Bertha?"

"He did not ask me, Miss Jessie."

Jessie swung about to see Mr. Blair talking to her mother. But although he was busily engaged with the Roselawn lady, the superintendent's gaze followed Bertha to the elevator, and that not idly. But the girl disappeared without the superintendent's speaking again to her.

Most of the professionals were already at the station, and the orchestra as well. Having sung and played for broadcasting before, Mr. Blair considered that they might rehearse in one of the smaller soundproof rooms without much attention on his part.

But to show the amateurs what to do and how to do it was an entirely different matter. The girls' chorus trained by the New Melford high school singing teacher was the number which threatened the most trouble. There were nearly thirty girls in the chorus, and now that school was over some of them were not very amenable to discipline.

Belle Ringold made considerable trouble for Miss Allister and delayed the rehearsal while she told, tossing her head, just how she thought the songs should be sung.

Mr. Blair was a brusk man and he stood for very little of this.

"If that girl is not amenable to discipline, Miss Allister, excuse her from your chorus. We cannot be delayed. Mr. Stratford himself and the ladies of the committee are downstairs listening in on this rehearsal. If it is not soon perfect I am afraid we will have to substitute something else for your chorus."

Most of the other girls were excited by this threat, and they promised to be careful. But Belle and Sally Moon pouted and shuffled their feet, and otherwise behave like naughty children instead of like high school young women. Miss Allister tried to hide their impoliteness; she knew them well. It was evident, however, that the rehearsal was going badly and that Mr. Blair was disappointed.

Jessie and Amy stood by anxiously, awaiting their turn to sing and recite. It was very warm in the sending room, although some attempt had been made to ventilate it. But the heavy curtains hung all about kept out the air as well as keeping in the sounds.

The singers faced a battery of receiving horns. The sound amplifiers were out of sight. Indeed, there was little mechanism to disturb the attention of the performers. The girls should have sung just as easily and nicely as they did in the school audience hall.

But the rehearsal continued to go badly. Jessie got as nervous as though she had been one of the chorus herself. And this was bad for her; for soon, she knew, she would be called upon to sing her own short ballad.

CHAPTER XVII

AN INVITATION TO A PARTY

SUPERINTENDENT BLAIR suddenly put up his hand and stopped the chorus in the middle of its second number. He looked very stern but he spoke composedly enough to Miss Allister. She was in a flutter of excitement.

"Let them rest awhile," said Mr. Blair, bruskly. "They are not doing well; nowhere near good enough to broadcast from Stratfordtown. We pride ourselves here, Miss Allister, on sending out good stuff.

"Perhaps they will do better later. Let them rest. Meanwhile, we will try out these others. Who is first? Miss Norwood?" He looked from the paper in his hand to Jessie.

"Oh, yes! Miss Norwood. Ready, Miss Jessie?"

Jessie gave her music to the accompaniest at the piano. Her hands shook and she flushed and paled alternately. She wished that she had a glass of water. Her mouth felt as dry as though she were suffering from a fever.

She caught, however, Amy's encouraging

glance. Amy never showed nervousness on such an occasion as this. She was perfectly calm. Jessie tried to control her trembling as she stood before the horn and the first chords of the music were struck on the piano by the lady who played her accompaniment.

Jessie Norwood had a very sweet voice and a strong one. She had something more than that, too—sympathy. When she sang anything it was with feeling and an expression that few but professional performers obtain.

Before the song was half through the girl from Roselawn had gained Mr. Blair's full attention and at its end he marked his approval by swift applause.

"Good! Good!" he ejaculated. "Now," he said, swinging to face the other girls, "if you young people would do half as well, your songs would be all right. Now! Who comes next?"

He looked at his paper and announced Amy's recitation. It was a humorous bit, that Amy did very well indeed. She had the ease that usually marks a much more practiced recitationist. After all, the full flavor of the piece was lost on radio telephony because her facial expression and her gestures would not be seen by her audience downstairs. But Mr. Blair had as encouraging a smile for her as he had had for Jessie.

The latter, in the midst of Amy's recitation, felt that somebody was standing behind her. She turned swiftly. Smilingly looking into her flushed face, and with his hand stretched out, stood Mark Stratford. It was the first time Jessie had seen him since he had fallen with his aeroplane on the Norwood premises.

He seized the Roselawn girl's hand and squeezed it warmly, but they did not speak until Amy had "made her bow" at the end of the recitation.

"Got to say Thank you! Jessie," whispered the young man. "You and Amy Drew certainly were good friends of mine when I fell that time. Sorry you were not at home when I called."

"Oh, Mark! We did not do much," said Jessie, flushing.

"That's according to what you call 'much.' To me it was much. I understand that I was in line for incineration in that plane if you girls had not dragged me out and put out the fire."

"Amy put out the fire," said Jessie, earnestly but in the same low tone.

"It's all right," and Mark grinned. "I know whom to thank."

"But, Mark! We didn't find your watch!" Jessie Norwood exclaimed eagerly.

"I suppose not. I suppose the place has been raked over for it?"

"Oh, yes. Amy and I looked carefully. I am so sorry!"

"Don't let it worry you. Of course, I'd give a good deal rather than lose it. I suppose it would do no good to offer a reward for it?" he added thoughtfully. "I don't want my grandmother to know. She is so old, you know, that she is easily disturbed."

Jessie was greatly disturbed, and she was not old! She stared at Mark Stratford with worried look. Should she tell him her suspicions regarding the red-haired Dogtown boy, Monty Shannon?

Mr. Blair just then was congratulating Amy Drew. She had finished her recitation and with a glowing face and a smile she came away from the horn. She saw Mark, then, and waved her hand to him. As he went to meet her Jessie was given a moment's time to reconsider the matter of the lost watch.

Jessie Norwood was no prude; but she did want to do the right thing. She had been trained to think for herself; perhaps she got a certain logical slant of mind from her father. And, in addition, she felt a real interest in Montmorency Shannon.

The red-haired boy was so bright and ingenious that it seemed a more than dreadful thing for him to be suspected of stealing. If he had found the watch at the scene of the aeroplane disaster and had hidden and sold it, stealing was the only term that applied.

"I must try to get him to confide in me," thought Jessie. "He must tell me how he expects to pay for that receiving set he says he has bought."

Mr. Blair nodded to Miss Allister then and told her to try the chorus again.

"I am going down to the reception room to listen in with the people there. I want to see how it sounds at a distance."

Amy of course began to giggle when she whispered to Mark and Jessie: "He wants to *see* how it *sounds!* Isn't that funny?"

Belle Ringold had fixed her eyes on Mark when first he slipped into the room; she could scarcely give her attention to the renewed rehearsal. Miss Allister was greatly flustered by the inattention of the girls. She had really lost control of them.

"Let's get out of this squalling," said Mark, in an undertone. "Guess that chorus is going to be a frost. That is what brought me up here. I was listening in with father and the ladies downstairs, and father sent me up to tell Blair that he doubted if the chorus would add anything to the reputation of the company, even if it was for charity."

"Oh, dear, me," murmured Jessie when they

got out into the anteroom. "If the chorus is not a success Miss Allister will be awfully disappointed."

"Not to say anything of how mad Belle and Sally will be," said Amy. "Oh, Jess! We are lucky that we didn't get into the chorus after all."

"You girls need not be troubled," Mark said kindly. "Your bits will stand out well in the entertainment. More individual, you know. And I think you both do mighty well."

He took them down to the big offices where the company's receiving station was situated. Here was an audience room seating at least a hundred people, and with the use of an amplifier and loud speaker the numbers being tried upstairs could be plainly heard.

Jessie was rather disappointed in not being able to speak to Mr. Blair again. Somehow, she felt that the superintendent was interested, in spite of himself, in Bertha Blair. Their last names were the same. Was it not probable that the girl was a relative of the superintendent? At least, it seemed possible.

There was no chance just then to speak of the matter. Her mother and the other women of the hospital committee were discussing excitedly the case of the girls' chorus, and how discordant it had sounded.

"I do not understand it," said one of the mem-

bers of the committee. "You will all agree that
at the school celebration Miss Allister had them
perfectly trained. I really expected them to do
even better here."

"Oh, perhaps they will be all right when it
comes to the night of the concert itself," rejoined
one easy-going person. "They are only girls, you
know, after all."

"But," declared Mrs. Norwood vigorously,
"they are old enough to realize that this is an
important thing. They should appreciate the op-
portunity to aid in a good cause. At least I, for
one, do not mean to see the girls make our concert ridiculous. I know what is the matter with
that chorus."

"Bully!" whispered Amy, under her breath.

"I think you speak rather harshly, Mrs. Norwood." It was Mrs. Moon who spoke. The
Moons and the Ringolds "always worked in
double harness," to quote Amy Drew. "Surely
we cannot expect the girls to take the matter as
seriously as we do."

"Why not?" Jessie's mother demanded. "The
hospital is for the poor and the sick among wom-
en and children of our town. Every girl singing
in that chorus is quite old enough to understand
that. You heard what Mr. Stratford said. He
cannot approve the chorus unless it sounds
better."

"I am very sure Mrs. Ringold will not agree
to having the chorus cut out of the program!"
Mrs. Moon exclaimed. "And I can see that is
what you are aiming at. If she were here——"

"Why isn't Mrs. Ringold here?" interposed
another of the members.

"She was too busy."

"Really? And aren't our private and personal
affairs just as important as Mrs. Ringold's?" was
the exclamation. "I approve of what Mrs. Norwood says. Give Miss Allister one more chance.
If the chorus does not show up better at the next
rehearsal, cut it out and find other numbers to
take the place of it."

On the way home in the Norwood car Amy
whispered to Jessie:

"Suppose they do cut out the chorus, Jess?"

"Well—if they do?" returned her chum.

"What I said before. We might get better
parts. And get Nell Stanley into it, too."

"Oh, goody!" exclaimed Jessie, suddenly clap-
ping her hands. "And there is Bertha, too."

"Bertha Blair?" asked Amy curiously.

"Yes. She wants to sing there. And perhaps
she would be willing to sing for the hospital fund
and in that way get Mr. Blair interested in her."

"Mr. Blair—Bertha Blair. Humph! Funny,
isn't it?" drawled Amy. "But on the other hand,
there's little Hen who is Bertha's cousin. Guess

Mr. Blair is no relative of little Hen," and the gay girl laughed.

Oddly enough the freckled little girl was the first person they saw when the car rolled into the Norwood place. Henrietta, dressed in her mended taffeta silk and silk stockings, stood on the lower step of the house eagerly looking down the drive. The Roselawn girls had not seen her since the week of the *Water Thrush.*

"Oh, Miss Jessie!" she cried when Chapman had brought the car to a halt. "I got an invite for you; and for Miss Amy, too."

"An 'invite'?" asked Jessie, somewhat puzzled.

"Yep. It's coming off to-night. Mrs. Foley almost forgot it."

"What did she almost forget?" Jessie pursued, while, as usual, Amy broke into laughter.

" 'Tain't nothing to laugh at," declared the odd child. "But having six—and all boys—it's not to be wondered at."

"Do tell us what it is you are trying to say?" begged the amused Jessie. "And what have Mrs. Foley and her six boys got to do with it?"

"Everything," said Henrietta promptly. "Anyway, Billy has something to do with it. It's his birthday and his party you're invited to."

"Oh, my goodness!" cried Amy. "Now I understand. Billy Foley is to have a birthday party."

"That's what I said," declared Henrietta complacently. "And Mrs. Foley says if you two young ladies was to come it would please her highly."

It was evident that the invitation was couched very nearly in Mrs. Foley's own words. Jessie and Amy looked at each other and by eye-signal agreed.

"Of course we will come, Henrietta," said Jessie. "And we are very glad that Mrs. Foley thought of us."

CHAPTER XVIII

BILLY'S BIRTHDAY

DARRY and Burd had towed in the *Water Thrush* while the girls had gone to Stratfordtown with Mrs. Norwood; but they were so busy caulking the seams and repainting the launch that Jessie and Amy could not look to the young collegians for any companionship that afternoon.

"And we mustn't annoy them—the way Belle and Sally Moon do," said Jessie.

"I like that! My own brother," sniffed Amy. "He needn't think he's so big just because he goes to Yale."

"We don't want to get snubbed, do we?" laughed her chum. "Come on, honey. I've an errand down at Brill's. He's got a new kind of a test-buzzer, and I want to try it, and buy one if it is better than our old one. You know, Brill has got a set in working order and you can listen in down there just as though you were at home here."

"Goody!" proclaimed Amy. "I was just feeling like a George Washington sundae."

"Dear me! How much you think of the inner man, Amy," sighed Jessie.

"Don't talk so wildly," admonished her chum. "It is the inner girl I am thinking of, I assure you. Wait till I run and get my purse," she added. "I don't want to lead you into the Dainties Shop again without being well supplied with cash."

They went to the radio place first, and after seeing the buzzer tried out, Jessie bought one. She was always on the lookout for improved parts for her set. Daddy Norwood laughingly said that it cost as much to keep Jessie's radio up to date as it did to support their two automobiles.

That, however, was "stretching the point" a good deal. Nor need one have as expensive a set as Jessie Norwood had, or as many expensive parts, if the enthusiast is limited in capital.

"If Monty Shannon can get a whole big set for fifteen dollars," Amy observed as they left the Brill store, "almost anybody might become a radioite."

Jessie sighed. "I am worried about that," she confessed. "When we go over to Dogtown to-night we must try to get that boy to tell us how he got money for his set."

"I've asked him already," Amy said. "But he is foxy. There is something mysterious about it, that is sure."

The girls went along to the Dainties Shop of

which Amy, at least, was a very good patron. She hurried ahead and, had she not been so quick in running down the steps into the place, Jessie would have held back.

"Oh, Amy!" the latter murmured. "There's Belle and Sally."

But Amy had pushed open the screen door. "Come on!" she whispered fiercely, looking back at her chum. "I won't back out now."

So Jessie followed her down the steps and into the pretty shop. Several of the tables were occupied. Right near the door were the girls Jessie had spied—Belle and Sally.

"Hullo, children!" said Amy, cheerfully. "What are you eating that's good?"

"It doesn't matter," Belle said sharply. "We have given our order already."

"Dear me, Belle," the incorrigible Amy said calmly, "you don't suppose that I expected generosity from you? Never!"

"You'll get something from me you don't expect," muttered Belle. "You and Jess Norwood think you are wonderful, don't you? Those silly little things you did over there at the rehearsal will never make a hit on the program. Don't think it."

"My mother," said Sally Moon, "said she could hardly hear Jess singing; and that piece you recited, Amy, is as old as the hills."

Jessie said nothing, but her chum was not to be so easily browbeaten. She tossed her head and laughed.

"That's all right, Sally. If Jess and I did no better than your chorus we would have been put off the program right then and there. You girls have got another chance; but you'd better be careful."

"Is that so?" cried Belle in her ugliest manner. "I suppose you know so much about it because you are friendly with Mark Stratford. He fell in your yard, and so you know him," and she laughed. "And I understand it cost him his gold watch and chain to fall there."

"Why, Belle!" gasped Jessie. "You shouldn't say that."

"Who is going to stop me, I'd like to know?" returned the girl of the unhappy temper. "You are not my boss."

"And I guess Miss Allister has made up her mind she isn't your boss," interposed Amy, who could not be as patient as her chum. "The poor woman!"

"I wish you'd mind your own affairs," Belle said, her face blazing. "If that chorus is cut out of the radio program we'll know whom to thank. And if it *is* cut out—well, you Roselawn girls will find out something, I guess."

"That is what we are here for," admitted Amy. "To learn."

She went along to an empty table and Jessie followed her. The latter was much more seriously troubled by the encounter than Amy.

"What do you suppose Belle and Sally mean to do? They may entirely wreck that chorus," Jessie said.

"Let 'em," said her chum. "If the chorus is cut out of the program we'll have a better chance. And Nell, too."

"But it seems too bad about the other girls. They are not all like Belle and her friends."

"Those Ringolds are always up to something tricky," said Amy. "I shouldn't wonder at all if Belle had got her mother to scheme some way of making trouble for your mother and the other members of the hospital committee, Jess."

"Oh! That would be too mean! And when it is for so good a cause!" Jessie said. "I know Momsy is very much worried about the concert."

"You see," prophesied Amy. "And then, think of their getting hold of the story of Mark's lost watch. We'll hear more about that before the thing is over."

"I mean, if I can," Jessie repeated firmly, "to find out something regarding that watch to-night."

Of course Darry and Burd Alling had not been

invited to Billy Foley's birthday party, but they drove the girls down to Dogtown right after dinner and promised to return for them later.

Henrietta and the Foley boys, with all their friends, were gathered on the platform before the door of the Foley cottage, and most of the grown folk of the neighborhood were likewise near by, the men smoking their pipes and the women with their arms rolled in their aprons, and gossiping mildly of neighborhood affairs.

" 'Tis proud I am to have ye here on me Billy's birthday, Miss Jessie and Miss Amy," declared Mrs. Foley. She rocked in a grand spring rocker, brought out of a neighbor's parlor, and one might think that it was her birthday that was being celebrated.

Mrs. Foley was a "bulgy" person who almost always had a baby on her lap when she sat down. But on this occasion Henrietta had relieved her of the youngest Foley and had popped him, fast asleep, into a box cradle in the house.

Billy, whose nativity was being celebrated under a fringe of Japanese lanterns on the platform, was cavorting about in an Indian suit, attempting to scalp all his little friends with a wooden tomahawk.

Jessie and Amy brought him presents, too; and they had been wise enough to give him "perfectly useless" playthings—the kind that delight a small boy. Henrietta brought him by the hand to thank the two Roselawn girls.

"I guess they don't want to kiss you, Billy," said the freckle-faced girl in her very practical way. "Your face is too dirty. Seems to me it always is dirty. I don't know how it is, but dirt just sticks to these Foleys. Even Charlie, big as he is, can't remember to wash behind his ears."

The visitors had brought hard candies for all the younger children, too. Most of the children played games on the plain before the group of houses. After being introduced to such of the grown folk as they had not previously met, Jessie and Amy joined the boys and girls in some rather boisterous games, for those were the only kind that the Dogtown children knew.

"You're a sight better than them other rich girls that come here from town," Henrietta confessed to Jessie. "You and Miss Amy ain't so stuck up."

"What other girls come here?" the Roselawn girl asked, with curiosity.

"Some like that Moon one, and another named Belle. They dress awful fancy."

"I know those girls. Why, you saw them over at the picnic the other night."

"Them's the ones," admitted Henrietta, pursing her lips. "They come here sometimes in a car to bring Mrs. Shannon fine laundry. But they never play with us Dogtown kids."

"No?"

"Did you know, Miss Jessie, that they are going to have another big time over at the old Carter place?"

"Another moonlight party?"

"Not like that one. It's big folks' doings, I guess," said the little freckled girl. "That Belle's mother and Mrs. Moon that sends Mrs. Shannon laundry, is going to boss it."

"I didn't hear about it," said Jessie, beginning to grow suspicious. "When is it to be?"

"Them girls was over here this afternoon and brought clo'es to Mrs. Shannon. They got to be done against the day the concert is going to be held at Carter's. It's sort of a lawn party, I guess; and them girls said they'd have a radio concert like you had over at your house once. You 'member, Miss Jessie?"

"I most certainly do!" exclaimed Jessie. "A radio concert? And when is it to be? Did you hear, Henrietta?"

"Oh, yes. It's to be next Wednesday."

"And on Thursday the hospital committee are going to broadcast their entertainment for the benefit of the hospital!" gasped Jessie. "How mean! The very day before!"

CHAPTER XIX

COMPLICATIONS

THE news that Henrietta Haney had inno-
cently dropped disturbed Jessie immeas-
urably. She could scarcely give her attention to the entertainment of the Dogtown
youngsters during the remainder of the evening
and until Darry and Burd returned in the automobile.

Little Billy Foley's birthday party did not end
until after the two college boys came back; for
they brought from the New Melford Dainties
Shop a big freezer of ice-cream. It was a generous supply, and immediately Darry and Burd
became quite as popular as Jessie and Amy.

While the excitement was at its height Jessie
slipped away to find the Shannon house. She had
not had a chance to speak with Montmorency as
she desired. Now she wanted to talk to his
mother, too.

"Yes, ma'am," said the red-haired boy's mother.
"Mrs. Moon sent me some things to do up that
she and the girl are wearing to the party at the
Carter place next Wednesday." Monty's mother

was quite as keen-witted as her son. "I take it the party is a secret yet. Yes?"

"What I have heard about it," confessed Jessie, "is rather disturbing. If they rig a radio over there——"

"It's what they are doing. They asked my Monty to go over and help string it. He has got what he calls his 'antenna' strung here and he says he'll have a machine in the house so we can hear folks talking and singing as far away as New York. Sure, I don't understand a thing about it."

"How will Monty pay for the machine?" asked Jessie bluntly. "They cost a good deal."

"Nor I don't know that, either," replied Mrs. Shannon. "But leave it to my Monty. Guess there ain't no brighter boy than him around Dogtown."

It was hard to believe that this woman knew of her boy's misappropriating such a valuable as Mark Stratford's watch. And yet, Jessie was still troubled by doubts. Before she left she asked Monty himself when he expected to get the radio set he had previously talked of.

"'Bout a week. I sent a letter and a dollar deposit, ordering it to-day."

"And it will cost you fifteen dollars?" the Rose-lawn girl went on.

"Yep," and the boy grinned. "I'm going to have a dandy. You wait and see."

"That is a lot of money for you to have saved, Monty," said Jessie.

"Huh!" and the boy grinned more broadly. "Who said I saved it? I'm going to *get* it. Ain't that enough?" and he ran away to join some of the other boys.

On the way back to Roselawn Jessie told Amy and the boys of the secret Henrietta had divulged about the radio concert which seemed to be the plan of the Ringolds and Moons and others of their clique, to be held on the following Wednesday.

"Why, it can't be!" Amy cried. "Even they wouldn't do such a mean thing."

"What do you mean—'radio concert'? They are not going to broadcast an entertainment such as your mother is planning, are they?" asked Darry Drew. "They would not let them do that over at Stratfordtown."

"No, no," sighed Jessie. "It will be a local affair, of course. But if they advertise it, and say it is for the hospital, and use the word 'radio,' people will get the two affairs mixed.

"The ladies of the committee wanted to interest as many people, far and wide, as possible, and Doctor Stanley will accentuate the need of large and small contributions for the building fund. If Mrs. Ringold's crowd starts anything in opposition, even if it is for the same good object, in the end it will do harm. I am sure mother's committee will see it that way."

"Sure," said Burd. "If they don't all pull together people will think the hospital will be run that same way. And that spells failure. How do those Ringolds and Moons get that way?"

"You answer that question; you asked it," sniffed Amy. "You don't know the half of it, Burd."

In the morning Amy ran over early from her house, waving a printed bill in her hand, and called up to Jessie from under the "radio window." Jessie was only then dressing, for she had remained up until late the night before telling Momsy and Daddy Norwood all about Billy Foley's party. She came to lean upon the window sill and looked down at her chum.

"What is the matter with you, honey?" she asked. "You sound just as you did the other night when the *Water Thrush* started to go down."

"It is because of that old leaky tub that I am here," declared Amy vigorously. "The boys went down town in the second car this morning for some new rope and hardware for the launch. Darry is going to fix it up grand, and while he and Burd are off on the *Marigold* we can use the *Water Thrush*.

"I'll ask Daddy if I may," said Jessie quietly.

"I'm going to run it. Don't fear," said Amy carelessly. "But look here."

She unrolled the paper in her hand with a flourish and held it up so that Jessie could read. At this Jessie screamed aloud:

"Oh, Amy!"

"It's worse than that," grumbled her chum. "Burd tore this off the telegraph pole in front of the Dainties Shop."

In bold type was printed:

RADIO CONCERT

and Dance

For the Benefit of

THE WOMEN'S AND CHILDREN'S HOSPITAL OF NEW MELFORD

Wednesday Afternoon and Evening
JULY 19

At Carter's Grove, Lake Monenset

RADIO CONCERT AT FOUR AND NINE

Tickets—One Dollar

"Do you see what Mrs. Ringold and those others have done?" demanded Amy warmly.

"They are going to queer the real concert if they can. People won't give money to both committees. It is disgraceful! People are talking about it down town already, Darry says. I think it is too mean for anything."

"It certainly will make trouble," her chum admitted.

"And just see!" continued Amy excitedly. "It is my idea, Jess. Don't you see that it is my idea? You remember the night we were down there and I suggested stringing antenna and having a radio set and dancing by broadcasted music?"

"I remember you did say something about it," said Jessie.

"Of course I did. And that Belle Ringold grabbed it and took the idea home to her mother. That crowd would never have thought of such a good thing in this world," scoffed Amy. "I think it is too, too mean!"

This opinion was shared by most of the neighbors of the Norwoods and Drews. Roselawn as a community was interested in the hospital fund committee's work, and the advertised "radio concert and dance," posted for the day before the committee's broadcasted entertainment, seemed to threaten disaster. Mrs. Norwood confessed that she did not know what she should do.

"I always feel when I am half through such a

task as this hospital fund raising," said Jessie's
mother, "that I will never undertake anything of
the kind again. "Something or other—sometimes
several 'others'—is sure to arise to balk us, no
matter how good the cause may be. I don't know
what to say to the other women on the committee."

"Withdraw just as Mrs. Ringold has done,"
suggested Mr. Norwood, who was not of a politic
nature, if he was a lawyer.

"I can't do that, Robert, you very well know,"
replied his wife. "And I fear our entertainment
will go wrong, besides. That chorus——"

In fact, it was the chorus of girls led by Miss
Allister that next brought the committee trouble.
On Saturday afternoon the chorus had been called
to meet at the parish house of Dr. Stanley's church
for additional rehearsal. When the teacher
gathered the crowd there were several missing—
all of them being friends and associates of Belle
Ringold and Sally Moon. They sent verbal messages that they had dropped out of the chorus for
good!

"And what can I do?" cried Miss Allister in
despair. "There are not enough girls left to call
it a chorus. And they cannot sing the numbers
properly. It is a failure. I shall have to withdraw the chorus from the broadcasting entertainment, Mrs. Norwood."

But Jessie's mother and the other members of the hospital committee who had remained faithful to the good cause were at least in part prepared for Miss Allister's announcement.

"There is twenty minutes of time on the program to fill," said Mrs. Norwood, to her daughter and her chum. "You two girls do so well with your song and recitation, I am greatly tempted to let you do more."

"Do, do, Mrs. Norwood!" begged Amy eagerly. "And let us show you what a nice trio Jess and Nell Stanley and I have. I'll run and get Nell now, and we can try it in the Sunday School room. I know you will like it."

"You are a dear girl," said the worried Roselawn matron. "I'll listen to you in ten minutes and will bring some of the other ladies. We have another rehearsal at Stratfordtown on Monday. I hope you girls can fill the vacant place."

"Leave it to us!" cried Amy gaily. "Why, next to Madame Elva and the jazz band, we'll be the best numbers of the whole entertainment."

CHAPTER XX

THE RIVAL ENTERTAINMENT

AMY DREW'S confidence was communicated, in part at least, to her chum and to the minister's daughter. The three really did sing very well in spite of the fact that it had been some months since they had sung together in public.

But they tried the number over and over before Monday and on that day, when the three rode over to the Stratford Electric Company, they were able to please Mr. Blair and the ladies who listened in.

"I must say that I was afraid of that large chorus, Mrs. Norwood," the superintendent said. "It takes a well-trained group of professionals to stand before the cone and broadcast successfully. Now, these three young ladies do very well—very well indeed."

"And there is another you might try, Mr. Blair," said Jessie, diffidently. "She was here to speak with you the other day, and I believe she has a sweet voice. She might want to help the hospital fund, too."

"Who is that, Miss Norwood?" he asked.

"Bertha Blair."

"*What?*" he exclaimed. "I never heard of her. Who are you talking about?" and he stared at Jessie wonderingly.

"Oh, yes, Mr. Blair. You have seen her," said Jessie eagerly. "Perhaps you did not know her name. She came here to see if you could not use her in the corporation broadcasting."

"It might be," he said thoughtfully. "Many amateurs come to ask for a chance to sing or speak at our concerts. I certainly should remember that name," and he smiled faintly.

"Perhaps you remember how she looked. She was here when we all came over from Roselawn the other day, talking with you. I had known about her before. She is a nice girl, Mr. Blair— a working girl," and she described Bertha's dress and appearance.

"And you say her name is Blair?"

"Bertha Blair."

"Can you find her, Miss Jessie?" he asked, with growing interest.

"I am sure I can. She is out at service. She works for a lady here in Stratfordtown. I'll run right away now and look for her. Perhaps she can sing something good enough to get upon this program. I've spoken to Momsy about it."

Amy Drew ran out with her chum on this errand. They chanced upon Mark Stratford in the main office, and he immediately joined them and found out what they were after.

"Get into my car," he said. "I know where that street is, and the house too. Run you around there in a jiffy."

"Dear me! How handy you are, Mr. Stratford," remarked Amy. "You are a lot nicer to us than Darry and the other boys."

"You cover me with confusion, Miss Amy," chuckled Mark. "I'll begin to believe that I am almost as fine a fellow as this little chap who wrote in to the corporation about a radio set he wants to buy. Some kid, he is! See here."

He turned around in the driver's seat and pulled a letter from his pocket. He was still chuckling, but he said:

"Honest little chap this, I tell you. One of the bookkeepers showed the letter to me, and I fell for the kid at once. I mean to look him up." Then he began to read the letter in question:

"Stratford Electric Company,
"Stratfordtown,
"Dear sirs:

"I just got your letter about my order for radio set to be shipped c.o.d. but I find you will have to give me Terms if you are to sell me. Ime only 12 years old, as I told you before, and I saw your advertisement in a boy's paper some time ago but I did not have so much money just then. But I got my antenna strung right and a man said he would give me some money for my rabbits. He was to come for them last week and pay me cash for them rabbits. But he didn't come so I cannot pay the c.o.d.

"If you would accept Terms (say one dollar down) and a month to pay the ballens, I could sell my rabbits to the Butcher, all but one pair to keep for good. I am sending a dollar, which is all I got just now, and hope you will accept Terms. Please tell the Post Office to keep the set at the Post Office until I can come in for it and pay the c.o.d.

"Yours respectfully——

"Well, never mind the name," Mark said, still laughing. "But isn't that some kid? I'm going to look him up and tell him he can have the radio set. I'll assume his debt until he can sell the rabbits."

Amy laughed delightedly; but although Jessie was amused, too, she spoke thoughtfully.

"I think that is funny, Mark. I do! And it is nice of you to give a boy like that so much attention."

"The kids are all crazy about radio," he rejoined. "But you don't often find an honest little fellow like this," and he put the letter back into his wallet.

They drove around into Mellen Street, where Bertha Blair lived with a very nice family. Jessie

ran up to the side door of the house and found
Henrietta's cousin at some light work.   Of course
the girl from Roselawn had to speak to the lady of
the house before she could get permission for
Bertha to go over to the sending station for
rehearsal.

"Bertha is crazy about that singing," said the
woman, when the girl had gone up to her room to
change her dress.   "She is a good girl, but not
just like any other I ever had to help me."

"I believe she is a thoroughly good girl," Jessie
said.   "And she is very fond of little Henrietta,
her cousin."

"That child!" and the mistress laughed.   "She
was here once.   Bertha wants her little cousin
with her.   But I am not sure I could stand that."

Bertha reappeared, and Jessie thanked the
woman for allowing the girl to go.   Mark and
Amy received Bertha cordially, and they got back
to the plant in a hurry.   Jessie took Bertha at
once up to Mr. Blair, who was listening in on the
rehearsal of other members on the hospital fund
program.

"So this is Bertha Blair, is it?" he asked,
curiously examining the young girl.   "I remember
that you were good enough to offer your services
for some program, my dear.   Suppose you go
up to the sending room, along with Miss Jessie,
and sing for us.   Have you your music?"

"Yes, sir," Bertha said composedly.

The superintendent still watched her curiously. "I don't suppose that I have ever met you before?"

"Not before the other day, sir," returned Bertha.

"No. I thought not. Well, go up and try it. I hope you will succeed. And if you suit Mrs. Norwood and the ladies in this concert I will make use of your voice again."

Bertha was delighted with this promise. Jessie wondered if the girl did not think that Mr. Blair might be related to her, but the excited Bertha said nothing about it.

Bertha's try-out was perfectly satisfactory. There is an art in being able to sing or speak into a sending horn, but the girl was intelligent and quick to learn. Mr. Blair telephoned up from the receiving room that Bertha's song was satisfactory.

Then Jessie and Amy and Nell tried their trio again, and that went better the second time even than it had the first. When the girls saw Mrs. Norwood down in the offices, after the rehearsal was over, her pleasant face was illuminated with a smile.

"I am sure of one thing, anyway," she said, kissing them all, not forgetting Bertha Blair. "The entertainment is going to be perfect. Those other women may hurt our fund with their party at Carter's Grove. Indeed, I am very sure they will. But the broadcasted entertainment will be as good as has ever been sent out from Stratford-town."

"I'd just like to know what they mean to do down there at Carter's place on Wednesday," Amy said, on the way back to Roselawn in the car. "What do you say if we go down to-morrow and look on, Jess?"

"If Momsy doesn't need me for anything," her chum agreed. "But we have nothing but the little canoe."

"We've got the *Water Thrush*, haven't we? Darry and Burd are going over to Crompton to the ball game. They said we could go along. But I hate to be always tagging. I know they don't really want us."

"Wise child," laughed Jessie. "But I don't know about going with you in the *Thrush*."

"Don't be absurd!" cried Amy. "I can run that boat just as good as Darry."

"And he ran it into a log the other night," chuckled Jessie. "Anyway, I shall have to ask Daddy Norwood."

But Mr. Norwood had looked over the re-vamped launch himself after the boys had got through with it, and had tried out the engine. He was convinced that it was in better condition than before. He believed, too, in the girls being independent of the boys in their out-of-door activities.

"Jess and Amy should know all about such things," he said to his wife when she expressed some faint objection. "Girls should be independent in everything. If they are going to work to earn their own support—as most of them do—why shouldn't they be perfectly able to manage their other affairs?"

"I hope Jessie will not have to go to work."

"I don't know about that. I have some young women in my offices that I respect because of their ability to buff for themselves. I guess they are domestic enough for all purposes; but they will never be helpless, no matter what situation they may be placed in. I want our Jessie to grow up like that."

In any event Mr. Norwood would not stand in the way of his daughter and her chum having a good time. He observed Amy handling the mechanism of the *Water Thrush,* and so consented to the two going out alone in the launch.

Monday evening, however, the girls were not on the lake. They would not have missed the broadcasting from Stratfordtown for anything! At eight o'clock, or a few moments before, they were up in Jessie's room with the phones to their ears.

With the receiving switch open the girls soon heard the tones of Mr. Blair's voice as he opened the hour's entertainment.

"Stratfordtown Station to announce: On Thursday at two and again at eight p. m. our radio audience will be afforded a special entertainment of two hours' duration arranged by the foundation fund committee of the New Melford Women's and Children's Hospital. This entertainment will engage both professional and amateur talent of a high standard, and will likewise include a brief talk by the Reverend Doctor Stanley of New Melford on the needs and hopes of the new hospital. I thank you."

"He has a soothing voice," said Amy thoughtfully. "Don't you think so, Jess?"

"Did you ever notice that it sounds like Bertha's?" her chum returned.

"Hen's cousin?" gasped Amy. "Well, now! Aren't you the greatest girl? Because Bertha's name is the same as the superintendent's! Well, what do we know about him? It would be romantic if Bertha found rich relatives, wouldn't it? Then she could have little Henrietta with her all the time.

"It would not need such dreadfully rich relatives at that," rejoined the other Roselawn girl.

An Accusation

CHAPTER XXI

AN ACCUSATION

OF course, it was curiosity only, and Jessie Norwood admitted it, that started her chum and herself in the launch for Carter's place on Tuesday morning. They absolutely had no interest in what the Ringold and Moon crowd were going to do at the grove save that born of inquisitiveness. They really should not have gone.

The dead walls and posts about New Melford had been well plastered with those bills, a copy of which Amy had first showed her chum. A good deal of vitriolic talk had been occasioned by the advertised affair at Carter's Grove. But that it would attract considerable attention and detract from the hospital committee's entertainment by radio, everybody could see.

The *Water Thrush* sailed splendidly. Amy had had enough experience with her brother to be able to manage the launch all right. And the trip was a speedy one.

Before they reached the abandoned house the girls spied the old canoe they had let Henrietta and her friends use, crossing the lake ahead of

them.   Several of the Dogtown boys landed before the Carter house and the canoe was paddled
away again before Jessie and Amy arrived.

Montmorency Shannon was one of the boys
who had come over in the canoe and the Roselawn
girls saw that he carried a roll of wire and some
tools.

"They are going to string the radio antenna,"
Amy said with conviction.   "Well, that boy has
got his own fixed all right.   Humph!   There are
Belle and Sally Moon."

"Let us not have any words with them," Jessie
said.   "But I do want to see where they are going
to have the radio set."

"There it is!" cried Amy under her breath.
"It is not uncrated yet; but I bet you they mean
to have it set up on the porch.   The roof of the
porch is quite sound—if it should rain."

"They have got a two-step amplifier and a
horn," declared Jessie.   "They can get dance music from two or three different stations," if they
know how to tune in properly.   I—I am afraid,
Amy, it will be a success."

Amy giggled.   "That does not sound like you,
Miss Meekness."

"I feel positively *mean* about this," Jessie
owned.   "I want them to fail.   It seems just too
bad that people should succeed when their plans
are wicked."

But when the Roselawn girls stepped ashore their faces were composed and the girls they spoke to saw no criticism in their faces. A supply of small tables and chairs had been brought over from town and the open space before the ruin of the old Carter house had been swept and smoothed. The tables and chairs were to be placed along the two sides of the open space. There were several men servants from the Ringold place working here, as well as the girls.

Belle and Sally ignored the curious visitors. They were, in fact, more interested in what the Dogtown boys were doing with the ropes and wires they had brought. Monty Shannon was in charge of the stringing of the radio antenna.

"They got plenty of wire all right," Monty said to Jessie. "And all the fixin's! I tell you, it's nice to be rich. See the set they've got there on the platform? Ain't it a dandy? It must have cost seventy-five dollars, or more. It's a whole lot better than the one I'm going to have."

"Haven't you got your set yet, Monty?" Jessie asked.

"Going to have it. It's shipped. Got a bill for it. But—but maybe I won't get it for a while, after all," he added hesitatingly.

"Come on, now, Shannon," broke in Belle harshly. "We're giving you half a dollar for doing that work. You're not supposed to take all the time in the world at it."

Monty Shannon grinned knowingly at Jessie. "Ain't she the slave driver, though?" he said. "I need that half dollar or I'd leave 'em flat," and he went leisurely away to the work.

"Let's pay him half a dollar and buy him away from Belle and Sally," suggested Amy, giggling.

But Jessie knew her chum only said that in fun. They walked slowly back to the shore. A sudden explosion of angry voices came from where the Dogtown boys and Belle and Sally were standing.

"Well, I wouldn't trust any of you Dogtown kids!" exclaimed Belle Ringold. "Don't you try to hide any of that wire. We need it all."

"Hey! Who's doing this, anyway?" complained Montmorency, in some anger.

"You are supposed to. But I'm watching you, Monty Shannon," declared Belle. "And you need watching. The Norwoods' chauffeur told our chauffeur what you kids did up there at Roselawn when Mark Stratford fell in his aeroplane."

"What d'you mean?" growled Monty. "We wasn't up there when the old plane fell."

"But you and your crowd were there right after it. And if Mark Stratford lost his watch there I bet some of you Dogtown kids know what became of it."

"Oh! How mean!" gasped Jessie, turning back from the launch which she had been about to board with Amy.

"I don't know," said Amy slowly. "We have been suspecting Monty, too, haven't we? Only we haven't said anything to him about it."

"And I am just as mad with Chapman as I can be," Jessie added. "I know he does not like the Dogtown children to come around the garage. But it is an awful thing to think that because they are poor they must be dishonest."

The quarrel at the place where Monty and his friends were at work continued. Of course, Belle was angry because she had seen the Dogtown boy speaking to Jessie Norwood. She really had no other cause for quarreling with him.

Suddenly a shrill voice was heard shouting from the lake. The Roselawn girls instantly recognized Henrietta Haney.

"Say, Monty! Montmorency Shannon!" she shrilled. "Come on home. There's somebody wants you. Come on home!"

Charlie Foley and one of the other bigger boys were paddling the freckle-faced little girl directly toward the landing. Belle and Sally turned to look at Henrietta, as did the boys who were at work on the radio antenna.

"Now, what do you want?" snapped Belle. "He can't leave here now——"

"He's got to," interrupted Henrietta importantly, and scrambling ashore. "There's a man in an automobile wants him. He's got to go."

"I say he sha'n't!" said Belle. "He's paid for doing this and he's got to finish it before he goes."

"Ain't been paid yet," said Montmorency, grinning. "What does the man want me for, Spotted Snake?"

"He didn't say. Only he asked about your radio——"

"You attend to *our* radio," Belle commanded. "Don't dare go away till it is done. If you do, Monty Shannon, Sally and I will never bring your mother any more laundry. Will we, Sally?"

Her friend agreed to this threat. Monty scratched his head and looked troubled. Henrietta grinned wickedly.

"You better come along, Monty. That man's a flying man. We seen him once. And his plane fell over on Miss Jessie's place."

"Mark Stratford!" ejaculated Amy Drew. "I never——"

"That's who it is," said Henrietta.

"Ha!" cried Belle Ringold, in her sneering way. "I know what Mark Stratford wants of you, then, Monty Shannon. You'd better not go home."

But Monty was already walking down toward

the lake. He waved his hand at his late taskmis-
tress and said:

"If you can't wait till I get back, get somebody
else to string the aerial."

He hopped into the canoe and seized a paddle,
pushing it out from the landing, leaving the interested Henrietta behind.

"Well, of all things!" gasped Belle, in angry
amazement. "How dare he desert us in that
way?"

"He ain't very daring, Miss Belle," said little
Henrietta cheerfully. "You couldn't do nothin'
to Montmorency."

"I'll show him what I can do! But he will be
in trouble enough when he gets home. I'm sure
of that."

"That Mr. Stratford didn't look like he meant
to make Montmorency trouble," said the freckled
girl. "He looked real pleased when he was talking with Mrs. Shannon."

"Bah! You vulgar little thing!" snapped Belle.
"What do you know about it? And you are just
as bad as the Shannons—every whit."

"Oh, I'm worse!" said Henrietta promptly.
"Everybody says I'm the worsest kid in Dogtown. Why! I'm Spotted Snake, the Witch!"

The laugh raised among the other girls did not
soothe Belle Ringold's rage at all. She exclaimed:

"Well, I know what Mark Stratford wants

that boy for. He's heard about you kids raking over the ruins of that aeroplane. That watch Mark lost stuck to Monty Shannon's fingers, and I'm going to tell Mark so if he doesn't already know it."

A flame of color swept over Jessie's face and her eyes flashed, but for the moment she said nothing. She had been angered by Belle's speech and feared that she would say too much. Her chum, however, was not so careful.

"Mean thing!" exclaimed Amy, sharply. "You don't know anything of the kind."

But Henrietta and the boys Monty had left behind him began to cry out at this aspersion cast upon their friend.

"'Tain't so! 'Tain't so!" shrieked Henrietta, angrily. "We never seen no watch. I was over at Miss Jessie's place, too. Why don't you say I stole a watch?"

"Maybe you did," scoffed Belle. "One of you got the watch, anyway. Don't you believe so, Sally?"

"Of course Monty stole it," agreed her chum. "And I guess he'll find that is what Mark Stratford wants to see him about."

"Oh, you mean thing!" shrieked the freckle-faced girl, and she charged at the two older girls as though she meant to beat them. "You're the horridest things I ever heard of!"

But Jessie interposed and held the angry child back from Belle and Sally.

"Let her come near me!" exclaimed Belle. "I'd slap her face good for her."

"Of course you would," said Amy warmly. "You are only twice her size. "Come on, Hen. Come away with Jess and me."

"You boys come, too!" cried Henrietta emphatically, and stamping her foot. "You heard what them two said about Monty and all us Dogtown kids. We won't do another thing to help them."

"You're right we won't," agreed one of the Costello twins. "Come on, fellers. Let 'em put up their own wires."

"We will just leave you flat," declared Henrietta, her freckled countenance still ablaze. "You rich girls think you are so big. I'll tell Monty and he won't come back and help you, either. I—I'd like to tear your clo'es off! That's what I'd like to do."

"Never mind! Never mind!" Jessie urged, leading the angry child toward the *Water Thrush*. "You mustn't do anything so rude to them."

"Well, I mean to put bad luck on 'em. Ain't I Spotted Snake, the Witch? I'm going to make 'em awful sorry for calling Montmorency Shannon a stealer; you see if I don't."

"What will you do?" asked Amy, much

amused, as they all got aboard the launch. "What sort of spell will you cast upon Belle and Sally, Henrietta?"

"I—I'll make it rain to-morrow and spoil all their party!" exclaimed Henrietta earnestly. "You see if I don't."

CHAPTER XXII

THE WITCH'S CURSE

AMY started the motor and the *Water Thrush* drew away from the landing. Belle Ringold was so angry with the Rose-lawn girls and the Dogtown children that she ran down to the edge of the lake and shouted:

"You keep away from here—all of you! Don't you dare come back here. I'll show you——"

"Who made you the owner of the old Carter place?" sang out Amy, cheerfully. "Take it easy, Belle. If only you and Sally are going to be here, you won't have much of a party to-morrow."

Jessie was watching Henrietta, who stood on a seat in the stern of the *Water Thrush* and who went through some very strange antics, scowling all the while in the direction of the old Carter place.

"What are you doing, child?" the Roselawn girl asked.

"I'm putting the come-other on 'em. I'm a witch. I'll make 'em sorry they talked like that about Montmorency Shannon. He wouldn't steal a pin! They'll have bad weather, you see if they don't. And when they grow up and get married and have children, the children will have rickets. You see!"

Amy went off into a gale of laughter while the boys grinned. They were very well acquainted with Henrietta's ways. But Jessie shook her head and beckoned the little freckled girl to her.

"Do you think that is a nice way to talk?" she asked Henrietta. "I know you learn to forgive your enemies in the Sunday School."

"Yes, Miss Jessie. I forgive 'em in the Sunday School. But this isn't Sunday School. You got to take your own part, or nobody won't help you. Mrs. Foley says so. How d'you s'pose a little, homely thing like me could have got the best of all those Dogtown kids if I didn't make 'em afraid of me? They know I'm a witch and can put the curse on 'em."

"That is an awful way to talk," admonished Jessie. "And Amy and I won't like you if you talk that way. It's all right to play being Spotted Snake; but to use bad language and say ugly things isn't nice at all."

Henrietta looked at the older girl very closely while she said this. Her face fell a little for, after all, she did not want to displease the Roselawn girl.

"All right, Miss Jessie. I'll try to be good like you say——"

"Be it ever so painful," added Amy, who was listening and laughing.

"Just the same," the freckled little girl added, "I put the bad weather on 'em for to-morrow—you see if I didn't."

The launch transported them to the Dogtown landing within a very few minutes, and when they got there no automobile was in sight. But Montmorency Shannon, grinning broadly, was lounging on the dock.

"Hey! What did he do to you, Mont?" shouted the boys.

"You haven't got to go to jail, have you, Monty?" questioned Henrietta, with anxiety.

"Not yet," said young Shannon.

"Was it Mr. Stratford?" asked Amy, shutting off the power and bringing the launch easily into the dock.

"That's who it was, Miss Amy," responded the red-haired boy.

"What—what did he want?" Jessie asked with hesitation.

"Wanted to look at my aerial. Said it was all to the merry," said the boy, still grinning. "Guess those girls over there at Carter's will wish they'd let me finish that job."

"Do you mean to tell us that *that* is all Mark Stratford wanted you for?" Amy demanded.

"Well—er—that's about all. I'm buying my

radio set from the Stratford Electric Company and Mr. Mark came over here to tell me I could have it right away and pay him for it when I get the money. He is all right, that feller!" and Monty's face blazed with admiration.

"Why, I wonder if Mark goes around giving credit to all the boys who want to own radios?" marveled Amy.

But Jessie saw farther into the matter than her chum. She asked with interest:

"Have you got a pen of rabbits, Monty?"

"Yes'm, I have," said the red-haired boy.

"And you are going to sell them to make up enough to pay for your radio set!"

"That's what I wrote to the company. Mr. Mark, he got the letter. And he drove over here to tell me he'd give me credit till I could get the butcher to take the rabbits. He said he didn't want any boy who was so much interested in radio telephony to wait for a set. He's going to pick me out one himself, and it'll be a dandy!" finished Montmorency, in a glow of eagerness.

"Oh, Montmorency Shannon!" gasped Henrietta. "Then they ain't going to arrest you?"

"What d'you mean—arrest me?" asked the red-haired boy. "I didn't cheat 'em. I only asked 'em to wait till I could sell my rabbits."

"But the watch, Monty! The watch!" cried the freckle-faced girl.

"Hey, Spotted Snake, what d'you mean?" I ain't got a watch."

"But *he* had! And it fell down with him when he busted his aeroplane. And he lost it. And now they say we found it up there at Miss Jessie's, and——"

"Hold on! I don't get you," said Monty, scowling. "Who says I stole a watch?"

"That Miss Belle and Miss Moon," Henrietta said hastily. "But Miss Jessie and Miss Amy know you didn't."

Amy whispered to Jessie: "I feel condemned. Don't you?"

Her chum nodded, but she said nothing. She was watching Montmorency Shannon. His face expressed nothing but anger.

"Well! They're the mean things!" he gasped out at last. "I'm going to tell my mother and she won't do any more fine laundry for the Moons and the Ringolds! You see!"

"And you won't help them put up those wires, will you, Mont?" asked one of his mates.

"You're right I won't."

"I'm glad Spotted Snake, the Witch, put the come-other on 'em," muttered little Henrietta, but watching Jessie with caution.

"You are all right now, children," said Jessie, the boys and Henrietta having gone ashore. "I am glad you haven't to wait for your radio set,

Monty.   And when you get it all fixed let me know.   I want to come down and see it, and listen in."

"You come along, Miss Jessie," said the red-haired boy, "you and Miss Amy.   You'll be welcome."

But he did not speak with enthusiasm.   It was plain that he was troubled.   Nor were Amy and Jessie carefree as they went homeward in the *Water Thrush.*

"Mark was awfully good to see Montmorency," Jessie remarked.   "But what will he think when we tell him about those children being up at the house the evening his plane fell?"

"We'll not tell him," declared Amy, with conviction.   "Why should we?   It certainly isn't Monty Shannon who got Mark's watch; otherwise he would not have to sell his rabbits to pay for a radio set."

"But what has become of the watch?" groaned out Jessie.

There was a thunderstorm that evening which interfered with some of the radio concerts.   But Jessie and Amy heard again Mr. Blair's voice out of the air announcing the hospital fund concert on Thursday.   What effect on the drive for funds for the Women's and Children's Hospital the dance at Carter's Grove on Wednesday would have, they could only surmise.

After the thunder rolled away and the lightning ceased to flash there was still a drizzle of rain falling. When Amy started home Jessie held her back until she could find an umbrella in the hall closet.

"Pooh! I'm neither sugar nor salt," cried the flyaway girl.

"But your frock is even more delicate," laughed Jessie. "Hold this over you. It has by no means stopped raining."

"You're right. And it doesn't look as though it would stop for a week. Oh, Jess!"

"Well?" asked her chum.

"The Witch's Curse!" Amy exclaimed, giggling. "Maybe that funny little kid *has* put what she calls the 'come-other' on that Ringold crowd and their entertainment. I certainly do hope so."

The next morning the skies were still weeping, and little hope seemed offered for the afternoon and evening when the rival entertainment at Carter's Grove was advertised to take place.

CHAPTER XXIII

"DO YOU SEE WHAT I SEE?"

LET'S go down, anyway, and see what they are doing," said Amy eagerly. "The sun was out for five whole minutes just now."

"Perhaps it will clear off," Jessie said. "They will be so disappointed if it doesn't."

"Don't get mushy about it, Jess," advised Darry Drew. "They'd be only too glad if your mother's affair to-morrow proved to be a failure."

"Right-o," said Burd Alling. "I never could forgive and forget as easy as Jess does. You are too good for words, Jessie."

"You don't know how painful it is," sighed Jessie, but with twinkling eyes.

"Never mind nagging Jess," broke in Amy. "I want to go down there to Carter's and crow over Belle and Sally and the others."

"You do your crowing under your breath, Sis," warned Darry. "We don't want to start any neighborhood feud that will disrupt the whole of Roselawn and New Melford."

"And the Ringolds and the Moons will certainly have chips on their shoulders if it starts in to rain again," admitted Amy.

"Perhaps it will clear," Jessie, the optimist, said.

"I am still believing in the witch's curse," chuckled Amy. "I am going to give her one of the best dolls out of my collection if the picnic is spoiled. Henrietta, I mean."

"Why!" scoffed her chum. "You half believe that the child really brought about this bad weather."

"No," said Amy elfishly. "But I do think little Hen should have a job in the Weather Bureau when she grows up."

The two young fellows were quite as curious as the girls about the outcome of the affair at the Carter place. The entire neighborhood having been well plastered with bills announcing the entertainment, and its being given in the name of the new hospital fund, it was bound to create interest. Busses were advertised to start from the New Melford post-office as early as two o'clock in the afternoon.

The girls and Darry and Burd boarded the launch, however, and started down the lake about three o'clock. A long distance away from Carter's they could see the strings of flags and other decorations. Mrs. Ringold and her helpers had spared no expense in making the place attractive.

There were decorated booths and a host of uni-
formed servants in view when the *Water Thrush*
came near. But, as far as the quartette could see,
there were not a great number of visitors.

"It's going to be a frost," Amy said, with confidence. "I tell you, our little Spotted Snake is a
wonder."

"Oh, don't say anything," begged Jessie, as
they prepared to go ashore. "I hope you've
brought some money, Amy. We must all spend
some."

"Darry has got some," returned her chum.
"That is one of the uses of a brother. And even
Burd may have a little."

"Oh, I know my duty," grumbled the stocky
youth. "I am prepared to buy George Washington sundaes, or Kewpie dolls, or boudoir caps, or
lollipops."

They were met at the shore before they landed
by two girls with decorated "tags" which they
were asked to buy for the hospital fund.

"And for mercy's sake buy from me and Mabel
and nobody else," begged Jennie Pell. "This
party is going awfully slow. There haven't a dozen
people come yet, except those who are working.
Mrs. Ringold gave us each a hundred tags and
said we were expected to sell them all at fifty cents
each."

"We can't make folks to sell them to," groaned

Mabel Frost, "even if we can make those we solicit, buy. Thanks ever so much, Darry Drew!"

It could not be said that either Darry or Burd Alling was niggardly with his money on this occasion; but the poor girls who had things to sell swooped upon the party from Roselawn like a band of hawks on four helpless chickens.

"You can't blame 'em," said Jessie. "There's not a handful of people here yet."

"And it is going to rain again," declared Amy.

"It's one solemn time—I'll tell the world!" said Burd. "Look at Belle over there. She's too unhappy to quarrel."

That was a misstatement. It was proved later that Belle was quite as quarrelsome as usual. But just then she was busy on the porch of the old house with the radio outfit that had been set up there, and Sally Moon and Mrs. Ringold were with her.

"There is something the matter with that aerial; don't you think so, Amy?" Jessie said, looking up at the wires stretched from the corner of the house to a distant tree.

"What is wrong with it? Didn't Monty Shannon get it stretched before he left yesterday?" asked Darry.

"He most certainly did not. And he said he would not come back to help them."

"Of course they got somebody to fix it for

them," said Amy. "Anyway, Belle talked as though she knew all about radio."

"So do a lot of people," chuckled Jessie. "But sometimes it's only talk. She knows how to use the detector and put on the earphones, and all that. But I believe that antenna is rigged wrong."

At that moment there arose high words between mother and daughter on the porch. Mrs. Ringold suffered the same lack of self-control that her daughter so often displayed. The Roselawn girls now heard Mrs. Ringold say in a high-pitched voice:

"You told me you could run this—that you knew all about it. Why, I don't get a sound out of it, and when you switch on the amplifier it is just the same. You seem, Belle, to know absolutely nothing about it."

"I guess I know enough," snapped the girl. "You've bought a broken set, that's what is the matter."

"Nothing of the kind. Unless you girls have broken it since it was set up here. I don't see why you shouldn't be able to run this radio just as well as Jessie Norwood ran hers. You don't have to go to school to learn how, do you?" added the woman scornfully.

Sally Moon looked very much disturbed as she came hastily away from the porch. She caught sight of Jessie and Amy standing near and came over to them.

"I don't know what the matter is with it," she said abruptly, but under her breath, to the Rose-lawn chums. "And Mrs. Ringold is so mad!"

"What's she mad for?" Amy asked bluntly.

"Oh, everything is going wrong. You can see that, can't you?" complained Sally. "Anyway," she added, "Belle and her mother are always fighting."

This sounded pretty bad, Jessie thought; but as the voices of Mrs. Ringold and her daughter rose higher and they became more angry, the fact of their "fighting" could scarcely be denied.

"Goodness me!" gasped Amy. "She'll slap Belle in a minute!"

"Can't they get any action at all from the set?" Jessie asked Sally Moon hastily.

"Nothing but a scratchy sound—like a bad record on a talking machine," replied Sally.

"Atmospherics," suggested Amy. "It's a bad day, anyway. There's thunder in the distance."

"They have been trying for an hour," said Sally.

"It's the rigging of the aerial," said Jessie thoughtfully. "Look, Amy. The wires are a little twisted, but what is making the real trouble is the way those porcelain insulators are put on."

She started for the porch. Amy cried after her: "Better not! You'll get your nose snapped off or something."

"But it will be awful if they can't give the radio concert after advertising it," Jessie murmured, hesitating.

Amy was still opposed to her chum's offering any help. But Sally had turned and run ahead. She now called to the angry Mrs. Ringold:

"Oh, wait, Mrs. Ringold! Jessie says maybe it is the aerial that is at fault. Maybe she can tell you how to fix it."

The woman turned with some relief in her face, but Belle was by no means pacified by this interference. She blazed out:

"Tell her to mind her own business! She doesn't know any more about this thing than I do."

"And you don't seem to know anything at all, Belle," her mother joined in maliciously. "Do you know any more? Can you see what's wrong, Jessie Norwood?"

This was not very encouraging, but Jessie had been taught to be respectful in any event. She said quietly:

"I am not positive. But it looks to me as though a mistake had been made in the stringing of the aerial up there."

"If there is," snapped Belle, "you like enough

put that Dogtown kid up to doing it that way. You were here yesterday when he was doing it."

"Stop that!" commanded her mother sharply.

But Jessie could not endure this false accusation without defense.

"You know very well, Belle, that Monty Shannon did not finish the job. He was called home. Whoever rigged the wires after he left made a mistake."

"Now, don't interfere here again, Belle!" commanded Belle's mother, and she actually drove her daughter away from the porch. "If you can help fix this thing I'll be a thousand times obliged to you," she added, turning to Jessie.

Jessie called the boys to help and in half an hour they got the wires untwisted and the insulators properly placed and Mrs. Ringold heard plainly through the earphones. It was in good season for the dance music program that would be broadcasted at four o'clock from one of the sending stations.

But, unfortunately, there were very few people to dance. The few busses that had arrived from town were not half filled. And almost nobody had come in private cars or boats. Just before four o'clock the thunder became louder and the lightning more threatening. The quartette of Roselawn young people made for the *Water Thrush* on the run.

In the cabin of the launch they could keep dry.
The other pleasure-seekers had to crowd into the
kitchen of the old house, or into the motor busses.
The clouds shut down over the picnic ground and
for an hour the rain poured torrentially.

Darry Drew got into oilskins and went out
and started the motor. Before the storm held up
they were at the Norwood landing. They had
had a gay time after all.

"But," said Amy, making a little face, "that
Mrs. Ringold didn't even thank you, Jess. Her
being a thousand times obliged was a joke. And
Belle will never forgive you!"

"What does that matter?" returned her chum
cheerfully. "We did our duty, didn't we?"

"Believe me," groaned Amy Drew, "I never
could get so much satisfaction out of doing my
duty, and I don't see how you can, Jess Norwood!"

As they walked up to the house Jessie suddenly saw something that brought a cry of dis-
may to her lips. Amy stared all around, demanding to be told the worst.

"What is it? Is the sky falling, Chicken Little?" she demanded.

"That aerial! See! Didn't I tell you when we
fixed it after Mark's accident that I thought that
hook we drove into the tower window frame was
not safe?"

"I believe you! It's down, Jess. Dear me! We do have the worst luck! And see!" she added. "It's broken the branch of that small pear tree."

"It is that pear tree that has the bad luck," said Jessie. "It came near to being squashed when the airplane fell. And now——"

Suddenly Jessie emitted a shriek and started to run across the side lawn toward the small tree. A branch had been broken by the falling wires, and now hung half torn from the stem of the tree.

Revealed among the torn foliage was something that likewise brought from Amy's lips a loud cry.

"Do you see what I see?" she yelled.

"Is—is it *real?*" gasped Jessie, in wonder.

The two college boys came running up the hill behind them. Darry demanded:

"What's struck now—lightning? You girls are enough to give heart disease to an old fellow like me. What's the big idea?"

But for the moment neither Jessie nor Amy could reply.

CHAPTER XXIV

THE GREAT DAY ARRIVES

BURD ALLING usually had the appearance of being half asleep. But he proved at this juncture to be quite as wide awake as anybody. He uttered a whistle of amazement and flung himself across the little round bed and scrambled up the short trunk of the pear tree.

"Hey! Where are you going?" demanded Darry. "You'll break another branch of that tree, you big elephant! It's damaged enough already."

But the girls knew what Burd was after. They waited eagerly for him to reach for the object swinging from the broken limb of the tree. He gained his intent and slid back to the wet ground.

"It is! It is!" shouted Amy in delight.

"Oh, dear! And I almost believed one of the Dogtown children had it," sighed Jessie.

"Well, I declare! You don't mean to say that is Mark's watch?" cried Darry in amazement.

"That is exactly what it is," declared his chum. "I've seen it a hundred times. And anyway," he added, grinning, "there isn't likely to be two such watches kicking about the Norwood premises."

"Well, it beats my time!" ejaculated Darry. "How did the silly fellow hang his watch in that tree when he was coming down in his plane? It gets me!"

"We'll take it to him when we drive the girls over to the concert to-morrow," said Burd.

But at that Amy uttered a squeal and reached for the watch with clutching fingers. "No you don't, Mister Alling!" she cried, taking the watch and chain out of his hand with a sudden swoop. "Jess saw it first. *She* is going to give it to Mark Stratford."

"That's right," said Darry, smiling. "Maybe he will feel like giving her a reward."

"He most certainly will," his sister declared. "And I know what she'll ask him to do for us."

Jessie looked at her chum knowingly. But she said quietly:

"If you boys don't mind, Amy and I will return the watch. And I want to show it to Momsy and Daddy Norwood. It will be a surprise to the whole Norwood family, for we scarcely thought that it ever would be found."

"What you going to do about this aerial, Jess?" Darry asked.

"You boys might help us put it up again, if it stops raining long enough. We'd like to listen in to-night, wouldn't we, Amy?"

"Yes, indeed," agreed her chum. "Wait till I run home and put on my radio suit."

"Cheese!" exclaimed Burd. "Darry and I will do it while you girls are fussing-up. All girls are alike. They have to have a certain dress for every adventure."

"Just the same," laughed Jessie, "I mean to stay right here and see you do it. We don't want to get those wires twisted as they did down there at the Carter place."

"And hurry up—do," urged Amy. "It will rain again before you know it. The Ringold picnic is going to be an awful fiasco. Bless that Spotted Snake! I am going to beg another dress from Nell Stanley for her, and take her over to the concert to-morrow."

"That is a good thought, Amy," cried her chum with approval. "Better than a doll. Will there be time in the morning?"

"Sure. I'll see Nell to-night. Then we'll run down after little Hen early to-morrow. She will be delighted to see her Cousin Bertha."

"The goddesses from the machine!" exclaimed Darry. "They make everything come out right for their friends."

"Including the finding of diamond studded watches," added Jessie, gaily twirling the recovered watch above her head before she ran into the house to show it to Momsy.

It rained just enough that evening to spoil utterly the affair at the Carter place. The Roselawn girls heard afterward that the lights were put out and the radio and other things packed by eight o'clock. The entertainment was a failure. There was no use in trying to run the affair when nobody came to it.

The great day toward which the Roselawn girls had been looking so long and so eagerly, broke brightly. Amy said, with delight, that "the witch's curse" certainly had not lapped over upon this Thursday. New Melford was laughing about the Ringold affair, and it was not likely that Belle and her mother would soon endeavor to interfere with any plans of the Hospital Fund Committee.

Of course, rain would scarcely have troubled the committee, but the girls thought it was much nicer to have a fair day in which to motor over to Stratfordtown.

Amy had secured another dress that would fit Henrietta, for the minister's daughter often received gifts of such half-worn garments. Nell Stanley was a perfect housewife and made "the Reverend," as she called her father, such a good home that he never felt the need of an older person to govern his household.

"I know I have got something more suitable for that child than a taffeta silk," laughed Nell.

"She looked like a little freckle-faced doll in that dress."

Jessie was delighted with the pretty gingham Amy brought up from the parsonage. There was very little to do to it to make it fit Henrietta, and the girls did that little while they sat listening to the radio telephone.

In the morning the boys drove them over to Dogtown through the bright sunshine and they "borrowed" little Hen for the day. The pretty new frock delighted her. She put it on, and then marched out across the platform of the cottage in full furbelow, her hair in curl-papers and Mrs. Foley's ancient purple silk parasol held over her head.

"Be careful of that parasol, Henrietta," admonished Mrs. Foley. " 'Tis the wan remaining thing that I had on me wedding day to show off wit', that me man hasn't hocked. The handle is rale ivory."

"Oh, see Spotted Snake with the parasol!" shrieked one of the smaller urchins.

Immediately Henrietta stuck out her tongue and writhed her freckled features into a horrifying mask. "You look out, Sudsy M'Guire, or the witch will put the come-other on you," threatened Henrietta.

"Ain't she the smart young one?" said Mrs. Foley proudly to Jessie. "She's got 'em all scaret of her—me own byes like the rest. And they are all saying that she made the bad weather yesterday that ruined the party of them Ringolds and Moons," and the bulgy Mrs. Foley was left shaking in her chair when the motor car rolled away.

The Roselawn girls combed out Henrietta's hair and smartened her up with ribbons before they started for Stratfordtown. They likewise managed to get her to leave the purple parasol behind.

"I s'pose," she confessed, "that I'd better not wear everything I've got that's fashionable all on one day. But that parasol is dreadful stylish."

The party arrived at the Stratford Electric Company plant so near the time for the concert that they had no time to look up Mark Stratford and give him the watch. But Bertha Blair was in the anteroom at the top of the factory, and she was very much excited. Glad as she was to see little Henrietta, there was something that had ruffled her composure.

"Oh, I have the strangest thing to tell you, Miss Jessie," she whispered to Jessie Norwood. "Wait till the concert is over. I must speak to you."

"Is it about Henrietta?" Jessie asked.

"Well, yes; in a way. Henrietta is going to share in the most wonderful fortune! You never would have suspected it. Oh! Here he is."

Mr. Blair entered the room and Bertha nodded

gaily to him. Jessie thought that the usually grave superintendent of the broadcasting station had an expression on his face different from his usual look.

But as Bertha said, there was no time then to discuss any matter. The hour set for the sending of the entertainment struck. They entered the sending room. Mr. Blair stood before a big horn and announced the nature of the charity for which the entertainment was to be given, and in which he hoped all the radio enthusiasts listening in would become interested to the amount of such contributions as they could afford.

The entertainment was divided into two halves. Madame Elva, one of the Roselawn girls' favorite professional performers, sang a group of three songs in the first half; and soon after this it came Jessie's turn to sing her short ballad. The girl was rather frightened when her turn came. Although she could not see the great audience that was listening in at this hour, she realized that Madame Elva herself and several other professionals were in the sending room.

Jessie had preferred to stand before the sending horn rather than sit in the comfortable chair that most of the performers occupied when they were sending. Mr. Blair came close to her and, leaning a little forward, spoke into the horn in deliberate tones:

"Stratfordtown Station: The next number on our program will be a song entitled 'Lily of Mine,' sung by Miss Jessie Norwood, of Roselawn. We introduce Miss Jessie Norwood."

For the moment Jessie was badly scared. It smote upon her mind suddenly that several thousand people were listening for the first tones of her voice. Although she could not hear or see her audience, it was there—and just as critical an audience as one in a great hall.

She heard the chords struck by the pianist; it seemed to her that she could not possibly find her voice! Jessie Norwood was afflicted with a pronounced case of radio telephone fright, which is quite as serious as the ordinary stage fright. She felt that she was voiceless!

CHAPTER XXV

A RADIO SUCCESS

THE chords of "Lily of Mine" seemed to ring hollowly in Jessie's ears as she stood before the sending horn. She flashed a frightened look across the room to where her chum, Amy Drew, sat beside Bertha Blair and Nell Stanley and little Henrietta. Little Henrietta was fussing with her hair and smoothing down the front of her new dress, and her face wore such a funny look that Jessie suddenly wanted to laugh.

This emotion shocked Jessie into keener comprehension of where she was and what she had to do. The pianist came to the point where Jessie should sing, and, scarcely realizing what she did, the Roselawn girl opened her lips and the first notes of the song came forth—clearly and in perfect time.

Afterward Madame Elva shook Jessie's hand warmly and smiled most charmingly in congratulation.

"You have a sweet voice, Miss Norwood," she said. "You will give it good care, yes? And when you are older, come to see me. Your voice has the promise of great things."

Jessie did not just then tell anybody of the prima donna's praise, but she was not likely to forget it! A little later Amy recited her humorous bit, and did it well. She was naturally a mimic. Bertha Blair sang with considerable success. Jessie saw that Mr. Blair watched his namesake with approval.

In the second half of the concert, after the band played the opening number, Dr. Stanley gave a brief talk regarding the needs of the new hospital, inviting contributions of whatsoever amount to the foundation fund. The clergyman had already preached sermons into the sending horn, so he did very well with this lecture.

Following this talk the three Roselawn girls sang their trio; and it was well done. Afterward they were told by friends at home that the tones were quite as clear and the song was as well rendered as any number on the program.

"One thing sure," said Amy, with satisfaction. "We did better than Miss Allister's chorus would have done. I wonder how Belle and Sally feel? They managed to spoil the chorus, and then their rival entertainment was a frost, and now *this*."

Mr. Blair was the criterion of judgment, however; and he expressed himself as perfectly satisfied with the whole program. He called it a radio success.

There was a social time enjoyed downstairs in the big reception room of the company's offices after the program was finished. But while the older folks were engaged there Bertha Blair told her friends from Roselawn of the wonderful news which had so excited her.

"So," she concluded, "he went back to where we used to live when I was a little girl—and where Hen's folks lived, too—and he found out that my father was his younger brother. And he is an awfully nice man, and his wife is nice, too. She's my aunt. And she wants me to come and live with them and not work out any more. And I am going to take Hen with me."

"Is she my aunt?" demanded Henrietta, composedly.

"We-ell, sort of," said Bertha.

"I can come and see Miss Jessie and Miss Amy once in a while, can't I?"

"Of course you can."

"And the Foleys?" demanded the freckle-faced girl.

"And the Foleys."

"I guess I'll have to take Mrs. Foley's purple parasol back," said the child. "You ain't seen that, Bertha. It's awful stylish."

Here Amy Drew broke in:

"I think it is wonderful, Bertha," she said. "And Mr. Blair is an awfully nice man."

"I somehow felt that you were related to him, from the beginning," Jessie remarked.

"He lost track of my father. They had a sort of quarrel when my father and mother married. And I guess Uncle Steve has always been sorry about it. He says he is going to make it up to me, whatever that means."

"I think everything has turned out wonderfully," said Nell Stanley, as the party broke up. "I don't suppose we shall ever have anything more important to do with radio telephony, or radio *any*-phone, such as we have had here at Stratfordtown."

Her friends, Jessie and Amy, could not disagree with her statement, for they could not see into the future any more than could the clergyman's daughter. But without equaling the clairvoyant qualities supposed to be possessed by "Spotted Snake, the Witch," we may announce right here that the Roselawn girls and their friends will be met again, in the next volume, entitled "The Radio Girls on Station Island; Or, The Wireless From the Steam Yacht," in which their radio experiences will be greatly extended.

Darry and Burd had hunted up Mark Stratford and brought him around to the car before the girls were ready to go home. As Burd declared, they had "worked Mark all up" over something good that was going to happen to him.

"I'm due to get something good," the young man declared, smiling. "I just got the bill for the work of rebuilding my aeroplane. And believe me! I might as well have bought a new one. Then, losing that watch grandmother gave me——"

"Ah-ha!" cried Amy, with delight. "Are you going to make some reckless offer of reward for the return of that watch, Mark Stratford?"

"Hey! Look here!" interrupted Henrietta. "You needn't think Monty Shannon, or none of the rest of us Dogtown kids, took your old watch."

"Never dreamed of such a thing!" declared Mark, smiling at the little girl. "I certainly would not accuse that Shannon kid of doing such a thing."

"You are quite right," said Jessie. "And to save you from further worry——" She proceeded to open the box she carried and handed him the watch and chain. A watchmaker in New Melford had cleaned and repaired the timepiece and it was running, as good as new.

"Three cheers!" exclaimed Mark, his face revealing his delight. "I don't mind the aeroplane bill now. You girls are wonders!"

"You ought to thank them publicly," said

Darry, grinning. "You've advertised the loss of the watch enough, Mark."

"I'll do it! I'll sure do it!" declared Mark, nodding.

But the Roselawn girls did not dream what he meant until the next evening when, at eight o'clock, just at the beginning of the Stratford-town sending station entertainment, and when Jessie and Amy had adjusted their earphones to listen in, they caught Mark's voice out of the air. It said deliberately:

"Stratfordtown Station: Before our regular program this evening, Mr. Mark Stratford wishes publicly to thank Miss Amy Drew and Miss Jessie Norwood, of Roselawn, for the discovery and return of a keepsake of which Mr. Stratford thinks highly, and for which there could be no possibility of adequate replacement."

"I declare, Jess Norwood! you are blushing," laughed Amy, pulling off her eartabs.

"It seems so public!" murmured her chum.

"I should hope so! Radio telephony is a very public thing, if anybody should ask you. See what it has already done for the hospital fund. In answer to Doctor Stanley's appeal, contributions have been pouring in all day. And it has only begun. Why, one of the richest men in this county had not heard of the charity until the entertainment started yesterday over his radio. And

he has promised ten thousand dollars.   While
four boys who own a set together in New York
have sent a dollar—a quarter apiece. Of course
it is public!"

"Hush!" Jessie begged, but smiling. "Listen in
again, Amy. Madame Elva is going to sing 'My
Old Kentucky Home.' Listen!"

And then all sounds ceased in Jessie Norwood's
sitting room save those which came over the
wireless.

THE END

THE EVERY GIRL'S SERIES

Helen in the Editor's Chair

By RUTHE S. WHEELER

"Helen in the Editor's Chair" strikes a new note in stories for girls. Its heroine, Helen Blair, is typical of the strong, self-reliant girl of today. When her father suffers a breakdown and is forced to go to a drier climate to recuperate, Helen and her brother take charge of their father's paper, the *Rolfe Herald*. They are faced with the problem of keeping the paper running profitably and the adventures they encounter in their year on the *Herald* will keep you tingling with excitement from the first page to the last.

Jane, Stewardess of the Airlines

By RUTHE S. WHEELER

We feel positive that this book is going to be the best girl's story we have ever published. Air travel has created an entirely new profession for girls, and it goes without saying that these hostesses have the thrilling and romantic experiences young girls will want to read about. The story is "chock-full" of adventure. From the time Jane Cameron obtains her position as stewardess on a large air transport, her experiences with passengers, the thrills of meeting movie stars and other celebrities becomes more and more exciting, until Jane, herself, gets into the movies.

S. W. F. Club

By CAROLINE E. JACOBS

The S. W. F. Club is the brightest, cheeriest, most wholesome of stories which tells of the doings of three sisters—Pauline, the practical, Hilary, the delicate, and Patience, the irrepressible—who live in the little town of Winton. As these girls cannot afford to go away for their summer vacation, they form the S. W. F. Club—Seeing Winton First—and with their friends have the dandiest times at their home town, which they find is not so pokey as they had at first supposed. The way Miss Jacobs tells of their jolly doings is bound to charm everyone who picks up the book.

Cheer Leader

By JANET SINGER

Anne Benson, a Junior in the Oxford high school, has set her heart on winning the coveted position of "Head Cheer Leader." Although this seems a simple enough desire, Anne finds herself involved in a series of baffling adventures in trying to attain it—including the machinations of a gang of professional gamblers, and the mysterious kidnapping of the football team's star fullback. It is a quick-moving, vital story that will appeal to every American girl.

THE GOLDSMITH PUBLISHING CO.
CHICAGO

THE MERRIWEATHER GIRLS SERIES
By LIZETTE EDHOLM

The Merriweather girls, Bet, Shirley, Joy and Kit are four fun-loving chums, who think up something exciting to do every minute.

The romantic old Merriweather Manor is where their most thrilling adventures occur. The author has given us four exceptional titles in this series—absorbing mysteries and their solutions, school life, horseback riding, tennis, and adventures during their school vacations.

CAMPFIRE GIRLS SERIES
By MARGARET PENROSE

These stories take in the activities of several bright girls who become interested in all present day adventures.

THE PEGGY STEWART SERIES
By GABRIELLE E. JACKSON

Against the colorful background of Annapolis and a picturesque southern estate, Gabrielle E. Jackson paints the human and lovely story of a human and lovely girl. Real girls will revel in this wholesome tale and its enchanting telling.

THE DOROTHY DIXON AIR MYSTERY SERIES
By DOROTHY WAYNE

Dorothy Wayne is the wife of Lieut. Noel Sainsbury, Jr., author of our famous "Bill Bolton Naval Aviation Series." The same characters appear in this air mystery series that appear in the "Bill Bolton Series" and because girls of today enjoy reading their brothers' books we have had these stories written by this outstanding author who knows how to tell girls the thrilling stories of flying, mystery and adventure.

PEGGY STEWART
SERIES

By GABRIELLE E. JACKSON

Peggy Stewart at Home

Peggy Stewart at School

Peggy, Polly, Rosalie, Marjorie, Natalie, Isabel, Stella and Juno-girls all of high spirits make this Peggy Stewart series one of entrancing interest. Their friendship, formed in a fashionable eastern school, they spend happy years crowded with gay social affairs. The background for these delightful stories is furnished by Annapolis with its naval academy and an aristocratic southern estate.

The Goldsmith Publishing Co.
CHICAGO, ILL.

RED STAR CLASSICS

Boys and girls the world over worship these "Classics" of all times, and no youth is complete without their imagination-stirring influence. They are the time-tested favorites loved by generations of young people.

The Goldsmith Publishing Company
CHICAGO